DEEP FREEZE

H. WALTER WHYTE

MANOR
BOOKS
INC.

A MANOR BOOK

Manor Books, Inc.
432 Park Avenue South
New York, New York 10016

ISBN CODE 0-532-12527-4

THE TIP OF
THE ICEBERG

I feel waves of grogginess flow over me. I am waking, I suspect, from a deep sleep. With my eyes closed, in this state of semi-consciousness, I try to recall the time which has passed. I remember the sense of melting into a pool. Sensation ended abruptly with a light going out and darkness falling over my mind.

Then there is a dream. And I seek in the dream to find an answer. I dream of the Arctic. I am lying on an iceberg, arms and legs buried in snow. In the distance is a great white polar bear. The bear is coming towards me, slowly at first, then more quickly; finally he is running. Soon he is standing over me, his mouth wide open and his hot breath panting in my face. At that instant I feel fear and a terrible numbness from the cold and the lurching sense that I am asleep and dreaming and must awaken.

But in a moment the bear has disappeared. I am still lying on the iceberg, and the iceberg is sailing down a steaming jungle river, melting away into the mud. Again I feel fear. I am afraid that the floating iceberg will disintegrate and I will be left unprotected, to be eaten by the crocodiles approaching from either shore. Their teeth glisten in the moonlight.

Just as the iceberg starts breaking into small pieces, I hear a motor and the sound of voices, and I know that I am waking from a very deep sleep indeed.

PART 1: THE COMING OF THE ICE AGE:
1978

I

New York/June 30, 1978/10:40 A.M.

"Hays Syndrome."

The words charge out of the telephone at my ear. I tighten my grasp on the receiver. Am I attempting, like the ancients, to wring the neck of the messenger of bad tidings?

"There's nothing that can be done for it, is there, Doctor?" I hear the echo of my voice, the hollowness of the words. It is barely a question. Last Thursday he had made it clear, painfully clear, that if the suspected diagnosis was confirmed by the tests, there was no cure for me.

Across the telephone wire I hear Dr. Soames

explain the death sentence. "I'm afraid, Mr. Minton, all three tests were positive," he says. I listen for sympathy, a word of hope, an inflection of understanding. But all I hear are the detached dronings of the scientific technician.

"There's no question but that it's Hays Syndrome," Soames continues, "I might say that I've shown the test results to several of my colleagues, and there was quite a bit of excitement. It's such a rare thing; one of those things you just read about in the textbooks. We'll watch you closely, possibly prepare an article or two for the medical journals, if you don't mind, and of course we'll see to it that you are as comfortable as possible . . . " The voice trails off. It is a whine.

"Thank you, Doctor, thank you for the news," I say. The conversation has gone on too long. I must end it. "I'll call you tomorrow." I feel the knot in the pit of my stomach tighten as I hang up the receiver. I have suddenly developed an enormous revulsion for Dr. Soames, for all doctors. I'm not going to let myself fall into their clutches. No, the Dr. Soames of the world aren't going to get me. If this disease means I have to die in my prime, at forty, better to do it without the benefit of medical ministrations.

The white intercom light flashes, interrupting my thoughts. It is that ever efficient secretary reporting on the half a dozen calls she intercepted while I was getting the report from Dr. Soames. She ticks off the messages: two land speculators looking for Minton money for deals they were trying to put together, a tennis partner calling about the new schedule for the club tournament, a call from the London office about progress on the Oxford shopping mall, and a message from Leland Anderson's secretary that Mr. Anderson had reviewed the Canadian contract.

Anderson, cool headed, cold blooded Anderson, surely he's the man to talk to at a time like this. Anderson is a lawyer, my lawyer, but he's more than an attorney, he is a detached intellectual presence, one of the few minds I have ever honestly respected. Perhaps, Anderson's quiet cool could be comforting.

"Lee, baby, I know you must have a date for lunch," I say when I finally have Anderson on the telephone. My tone is pleading, more pleading than I have sounded in thirty years or more. I catch the tone and reassert myself. "Break your date," I say, "I must see you. Meet me at the Four Seasons at one."

There is a brief silence at the other end of the phone, long enough to suggest sacrifice but not annoyance on Anderson's side. "Sure, Dennis, I can make it; but what's up?"

"Can't talk now, Lee. I'll tell all when I see you, baby." There is a quick disconnect. I realize that in talking to Anderson I have, without conscious decision to do so, buried the fear which gripped me. My ability to dissemble, to cover over my real feelings with the personality the world has come to expect, is suddenly exposed to me in all its full color. I wonder to what use I'll be putting that ability in the coming weeks.

9

II

New York/June 25, 1978/12:58 P.M.

I arrive early. I'm always early for appointments. It's a habit, maybe a bad habit.

Michel, that tall headwaiter who always seems to walk without actually letting his feet touch the floor, escorts me to my favorite table, the one in the far corner, with a commanding view of the large room.

I order a martini, dry, extra dry, and while I wait I scan the room for familiar faces. Suddenly the room depresses me. It is a galaxy, each table a solar system of influential executives. But the restaurant overflows with solar systems. Any one of them could be removed, the room would be no less full, the galaxy no less bright. My own unimportance overwhelms me.

The wave of depression is total. The arrival of the martini rescues me. The gin blurs the edges of insight, it makes the room fuzzy.

Then there is Anderson, tall, thin, craggy-faced Anderson. His meticulously pressed suit has a thin gray stripe, a perfect match for the gray at his temples.

"You're looking well," he says in greeting.

"It's as if he had thrust at me with a switchblade. The greeting sticks in my ears, it echoes. I gulp at my martini, drinking deeply from the large snifter.

"Sit down, Lee," I say, "something terrible has happened." I gulp at the drink again, this time finishing it. The glass shakes in my hand. "I have Hays Syndrome," I say.

Anderson bends forward toward me and frowns slightly. "What?" he asks.

In my preoccupation and fear, I have forgotten that the disease is an obscure medical oddity. I myself had never even heard of it until last Thursday when Dr. Soames first suspected the diagnosis.

The gin warms my insides, and the warmth pours over my body. I begin to explain slowly, "It's a rare disease, a virus, I think, attacks the nerve endings. It begins in a silly way, Lee, tingling in the toes. Can you imagine that?" I laugh weakly, and continue, "That's what sent me to the doctor last week. Anyway, Lee, there haven't been too many cases, but there have been enough so that they can predict the course of the disease. The virus seems to feed on the nerves, working its way through the system." I gulp again at the empty glass, straining to wring another drop of gin. "There's no cure." My voice becomes very soft; I look at Anderson and then out across the restaurant, vision blurring as my eyes fill with tears held back. I blink. "Lee, baby, I'm gonna die. Ten weeks, maybe twelve, that's all I've got."

In the silence when I finish speaking I suddenly become aware of all the sounds of the restaurant. They are magnified many times their normal level, the clangs of dishes and trays, and silver and people, a cacophony of small silence, and it nearly drowns out Anderson's hushed, "Oh, my God!"

Anderson reacts as if he has been hit in the solar plexus. He calls for a drink and a refill for my glass. This interruption gives me time to regain a sense of balance, of composure.

He immediately challenges the verdict. "You're sure?" he says. "Maybe you should see another doctor."

"No," I explain, "Soames made the diagnosis last week; he called this morning to say that three separate lab tests confirm it. He even told me he had reviewed the tests with some other doctors. Lee, they were all excited about it, like vultures. They want to write me up in medical journals." Talking about it puts distance between me and my real feelings, makes me more detached.

"Still, I think you should see someone else," says Anderson. He is persuasive, insistent. "You know, Dennis, in my business, if you lose in the district court, you appeal to the Circuit Court, and even if you lose there, you can still appeal to the Supreme Court. What kind of lawyer would give up on a case just because he lost in the first court? Well, it's the same thing here. I don't think you should quit just because one judge decided against you. Appeal the decision. Get a change of venue."

I hear the advocate pleading his case, but I shake my head in disagreement, and dive into the cool waters of that second martini.

Anderson continues, "Look, you're forty years old; you've been immensely successful in real estate, you have an attractive wife, you have everything to look forward to. If I were you I'd fight for that future; I'd go to the top men in the field; I'd try anything. In medicine there are always breakthroughs, new discoveries that old Dr. Soames may not be aware of."

I suddenly feel like a judge, before whom Anderson is making his crucial closing argument. I understand the source of Anderson's enormous reputation as a trial lawyer; in just a few minutes without preparation, he has been very persuasive. I smile. "Thanks, Lee, for the pep talk," I say.

But Anderson pursues the point. He won't

let it lie. "You will get another opinion, then?" he says.

I hesitate. I smile again and nod slowly. The court has decided in Anderson's favor. "I will," I say.

"Good," says Anderson. He moves his chair closer to the table and takes a pad and thin silver pen from his breast pocket. I witness a transformation. Anderson the advocate has left; in his place is Anderson the administrator. "Now who do you want me to contact?" says the administrator.

I am confused by the change in roles, by the no nonsense approach of the administrator. I grope. "I'm not sure I understand, Lee. What do you mean?"

"Aren't there people you want me to speak to, people you want me to tell?" he says. The pen is poised on the pad, ready to take down any instructions.

"No." I am frightened again. "I don't want you to tell anyone. I've told no one. I thought you should know since you're my lawyer, but I'm not telling anyone else."

"Not even Mary?" asks Anderson. I sense that Lee can not fathom my motivation for not wanting to tell my wife.

"No, I don't want to tell Mary just yet," I say. But as I speak I wonder how long I'll be able to keep it from her. I wonder how the deterioration will first manifest itself. What will Mary's reaction to it be?

"Of course you're entitled to your privacy," says Lee. "But time is limited. That privacy should not conflict with your use of the remaining time. It seems to me that you should have two goals: first you should do everything you can to find a doctor who can cure this thing. At the same time you should be making pretty complete plans for the possibility that Dr. Soames is right."

During lunch the problems are explored further. I see these as the alternatives of hope and despair. Looking for another specialist to disagree with the Soames' diagnosis or to produce a cure for the disease is the alternative of hope. I promise to tackle that one. Planning for the possibility that Dr. Soames is right is the alternative of despair. Anderson, the administrator, promises to deal with that one. Before we finish I thank him. He has helped; he has helped.

III

New York/July 8, 1978/10:00 A.M.

The old wall clock strikes ten as I open the glass door with the gold lettering. "Smoot, Baldwin, Blackwell & Anderson." As I sit in a green corduroy chair in the reception room, there is a twinge in my left ankle. It is dim, barely noticed pain, but it is there.

I try concentrating on the carved mahogany chest across the room, on the intricacies of its design. But as I wait, my mind turns to the deals I have closed with Anderson, the good ones and the bad ones. They've been mostly good. And we've made a lot of money, Lee and me.

I'm doing what I always do, pricing things. I put a price on the green chair, on the old Jacobean chest, on the elegant Kirman rug on the floor. What, I wonder, have I paid Smoot, Baldwin in fees in the last ten years, and how many of these lovely pieces of furniture have been paid for with my money?

The pricing game is interrupted by Anderson's secretary. She has come to escort me through the intricacies of the firm's interior. Without her I would be lost in a maze, perhaps never heard from again, among the whir of the electric typewriters and the reverse turns. Even with her it seems to take a full five minutes to reach the corner office which is Leland's and which identifies his rank in the firm. It is a northern and western corner, with full views up Park Avenue and across the Hudson to New Jersey. It is perhaps not as choice as the southern corners, but still marks Anderson as one of the three or four top men in the firm.

Lee greets me with reserve, even more reserve than usual. He stands, stiffly, offers a hand, but keeps the desk between us as he says, "Good morning, Dennis."

There is no small talk. He launches directly in, saying, "Since our lunch last week, I have given your situation considerable thought." He is upset, he is trying to conceal it, but it is clear. "I know, Dennis," he continues, "we agreed that you were to do the research in the medical field and I would limit myself to legal implications.

18

But I must tell you that I've done some medical research of my own."

I feel like I should do something to put Lee more at ease. I relax into the chair, hoping he will pick up the cue, and I say, "Well, lay it on, Lee, what've you got?"

Anderson seems to straighten in his chair. He has become more rigid, unmovable. He smiles, but the smile makes no sense in the context of the neat pinstripe and that perfect part in his hair. I realize that I have put up with Anderson, the person, all these years, in order to get the services of Anderson, the lawyer. And I understand, too, that the relationship has been symbolic, with Anderson putting up with Minton, the person, in order to get the legal fees from Minton, the entrepreneur.

Anderson fixes his eyes on me and speaks in the administrator's monotone. "I don't know if you remember, but my partner, Howard Blackwell had a neurological problem, that is his first wife, Julia, did. She was treated by a team of specialists in London. Howard did a hell of a lot of research and he found out that they were the best in the business. I spoke to him about your situation the other day. He checked his team out again and apparently they are still working, doing the most advanced things, chemotherapy, radiation . . ."

I smile weakly. The sensation in the left ankle returns, and I involuntarily rub my foot as I say, "Lee, baby, it's not the Foster-Belinsky group by any chance, is it?"

He nods, "Why yes, of course," he says, "So our independent efforts have both pointed in the same direction. I think I should also tell you that I sent one of the young men in the office up to the Medical Society library this morning to get a copy of Dr. Belinsky's article on Hays Syndrome. It seems to be the most exhaustive report on the disease."

"I've heard about it, but I haven't read it," I respond. The sensation, the tingling or twinge, is it, reappears, this time in the right ankle. I focus behind Anderson's steel gray temples, on the skyline framed in the window. I think about Foster and Belinsky and whether a visit to them might just be exposing myself even more thoroughly to medical journal immortality.

"I think you should see the Foster-Belinsky people as soon as possible," says Lee. He is in pursuit. The monotone has left and it is the old advocate again, warmed to the task. He pounces, "While you are here this morning I want to call them, maybe arrange an appointment for tomorrow."

I am impressed, moved, swayed again by the trial lawyer. I feel I have no choice but to agree; free will, denial, do not seem to be in the range of my abilities. I hesitate, then nod consent, saying, "You're the doctor."

"No, I'm not," says Anderson, indignation rising in his voice. Then he adds, in a softer tone, "I've been trying to speak as a friend." He pauses, and then, "Shall we call London?"

"O.K. Lee," I say, "Thanks." Ultimately the decision is mine, and I must take responsibility for it.

Anderson buzzes his secretary, giving her precise and complete instructions on placing the call to the Foster-Belinsky clinic.

IV

New York/July 8, 1978/7:35 P.M.

Lee has insisted on taking charge of all details. The call to London resulted in a 10:30 a.m. appointment at the Foster-Belinksy clinic for tomorrow morning. Meanwhile his staff has booked space on Pan Am's late flight to London and Lee is personally accompanying me to the airport in his private car. As we drive along the Van Wyck expressway I wonder what kind of bill I'll be getting for a day of Anderson's hand holding.

The car slows in traffic. Anderson is ticking off the things we discussed during the day, pending deals in Canada and Maryland and certain

23

aspects of the Oxford shopping center. I have told Mary that the reason for the sudden trip is a problem at the center which requires my attention; that is my cover. So after my appointment with Foster and Belinsky I intend to spend the balance of tomorrow visiting that site. Meanwhile Mary has been invited to come along on the trip, to do some shopping, and she is to meet us at the airport.

Anderson seems to be muttering to himself; the administrator rapidly going over the items requiring attention. Finally he says, more audibly, "Dennis, I think we ought to go over your will and estate plan. We never really had a chance to discuss that all day long."

Lee sounds cheerful. There is almost a spring to his voice. I feel my palms becoming wet; I rub them on the leather upholstery of the seat and reposition myself. My face flushes and I look away. I feel the tingling pain just beneath my right knee.

"Is there something the matter?" says Lee. He sounds concerned. "Dennis are you all right then?"

"I'm fine, fine," I say, but my mouth is parched and I am suddenly afraid that I am going to be sick in the car. I press the automatic window opener, but the fetid fumes of the outside air are more nauseating than the confines of the car and I quickly close the window.

"Shall I have the driver pull over?" asks Anderson. I sense concern, concern for his elegant car, concern for his well pressed suit and concern for his well pressed sensibilities.

"No, Lee, baby," I say, with more confidence, "I'm going to be all right." The wave of nausea is subsiding. Traffic has speeded up and the air conditioning is fuller in the backseat. "Wills," I say, "that's hard, it's a real hard subject."

As I talk, I realize that I have discussed my will with Lee at least half a dozen times, but those other times it was something abstract and distant, a game of chess in never never land. Now it is too real, too close, too final.

After a pause, Anderson says, "Are you up to it?"

"I guess so," I say. "Go ahead."

He begins in the dry monotone of the administrator, checking from figures on a pad he holds. The reading light is on to aid his vision. "The taxes on your estate will be quite substantial," he says. "Assuming a $7,400,000 gross estate, which seems a conservative estimate, and assuming you continue your present will provisions, total estate taxes will be approximately $1,200,-000." Anderson sounds like the Secretary of the Treasury, discoursing on the gross national product.

I focus on him long enough to say, "Lee, cut the garbage, what does my will say now?" Then I return my focus to a view of the road out in front of the driver, again almost bumper to bumper.

The administrator responds, "The last will

we did for you was in 1972. It puts all your property in trust for Mary. She has a power of appointment over the corpus, that is she has the right to decide who gets the property on her death. I am the Executor. The Trustees who administer the trust for Mary are myself and the Third National Trust Company, that's just in case Mary lasts longer than I do."

"So Mary gets everything. What do you think of that, Lee?" I turn my head to look directly at him again.

"Dennis," he says, "I think there are decisions here only you can make. Mary seems like a nice enough person; but it is your money, and quite frankly, this sort of thing has to be your decision."

I think about Mary. The car is approaching the airport road and we will soon be meeting her at the Pan Am terminal. My mind goes back to our wedding, ten years ago. She had been 22, attractive and longing for adventures. And together we have shared adventures: my business successes, foreign travel, the best restaurants and the best resorts. She has been an attractive companion. We have never had children. In the early years we were just too busy and recently Mary has become involved in her own business, as interior decorator.

In considering our relationship, I sense that we are really drifting apart. Given another five or ten years, the marriage may not last. But the will must speak for today, and for me, today, there is no one else, no one else I want to share the fortune.

"All to Mary," I say with some finality, adding, "I have no one else."

"You're forgetting about Barbara," says Anderson.

Anderson, the thorough administrator, has remembered. I must have once mentioned my first marriage to him, though I can't think when, and he has kept notes. "Barbara means nothing to me," I say, "I was married to her mother when we were both very young and immature, I wasn't more than 20. Barbara was born the following year and I divorced the woman two years later. I haven't seen the child in at least fifteen years, or longer. She must be almost 20 now herself."

"It may be that she means nothing to you," explains Lee, "but if something happens to you, she is entitled to legal notice. It's called a citation."

This explanation disturbs me. The tall observation tower of the airport is in sight; we will soon be approaching the terminal and the rendezvous with Mary. The conversation must be concluded quickly.

I think about half remembered Grade B movies with will contests and money hungry relatives. I owe a debt to Mary. I want things to be easy for her, as easy as possible under the circumstances. "You mean Barbara could contest, make trouble for Mary?" I ask.

"In theory, yes. As a practical matter, no.

You married young, this child, Barbara was born, the marriage failed fairly quickly and you were divorced. The mother and child were paid off in accordance with your then ability to pay. You never had a real father-daughter relationship with her. On those facts, and particularly since your fortune dates from the period after the marriage was terminated, no court in the world would give Barbara Minton the time of day if she tried to contest a will which failed to provide for her."

I am relieved. The car is approaching the terminal. "Then there's really nothing to be done about the will is there, Lee?"

"No, I guess not," he says as the car slows to the curb. "As long as it expresses your wishes. As it stands now, everything goes in trust for Mary, and she directs who gets it when she is no longer around."

No longer around. I smile. What a lovely phrase, I think, as we get out of the car. "Thanks, again, Lee, baby."

V

London/July 9, 1978/10:45 A.M.

There is something disconcerting about Dr. Foster's thick black eyebrows and his gray goatee. Or perhaps I am suffering from the fatigues of time change and a sleepless night on the plane.

I have little time to worry about the Doctor's appearance. No sooner have I met him, and his partner, than I am promptly led away by one of those fair haired English lasses. She is wearing a tight fitting uniform which takes my mind off time changes and the gray London overcast.

I am ordered to disrobe by the young nurse. The wheels in my mind turn more quickly. Then

I am told to lie down on the marble table in the center of the room. It is cold, unbearably cold, and damp. And drains all hope or desire. Straps are applied by the nurse, all the while chatting quietly about the weather and the states. Then she starts sticking pins, they are electrodes, she tells me, at joints and other sites around the body. The process takes several minutes. When it is over, I feel like a pin cushion.

The nurse leaves. I have a few moments a-lone, then as I lie still on the cold table, I feel a twinge of pain in my right ankle, just under an electrode. It is only a suggestion of pain, growing slowly until it disturbs the consciousness. Almost as I become aware of it, the pain subsides. Then it reappears, at my knee, beneath another electrode. And when it draws a response at the knee, it is gone, moving up to the thigh. The process continues slowly up one side of my body, even more slowly down the other.

The pain subsides under the electrode at my left ankle. I am alone in the room and strain my neck to find a window or other indication that I am being observed. There is none that I can see.

Then, without warning, the pain begins again in my right ankle. This time it seems slightly quicker to reach through threshold, and the intensity is stronger. I fix on the wall clock set a-cross the room. I time this circuit; it relieves the pain. At the end of eight minutes the pain has reached my left ankle, the circuit is over.

Again there is a moment of quiet. My palms

are wet against the cold marble, and I feel the beads of perspiration at my scalp. Then it begins again, again in the right ankle, and again it is more intense.

This time I squirm against the bindings. The pain is too intense. But it won't stop. It proceeds slowly up one side of my body and down another. When it is over, I smell burning rubber and I feel complete exhaustion.

Again there is quiet. Then, again the pain commences. More intense, it is still more intense. I have no sensation left. I scream, the sound bouncing back to me again and again from all sides of the tiled room.

Then I lose the sense of it. It continues, but I have lost the ability to quantify. I am at some semi-conscious level where the pain has a reality outside and beyond me. Then there is a void.

I suddenly find myself submerged to my neck in a clear green fluid. It smells and looks like after shave lotion. I seem to be in a stall shower, tile walls on three sides and a glass door on the fourth. The green fluid tones my muscles and seems to soothe my joints. Slowly it begins to recede. When it has reached my knees I watch the whirlpool it makes as it drains from this strange shower.

In another moment that attractive young nurse opens the glass door and covers me with a warm towel. "You may put on your things in the dressing room," she says. "When you are ready, just ring. Dr. Foster will see you."

I dress quickly. The cobwebs have been swept from my mind. I am not quite sure why, but I no longer feel the grogginess from lack of sleep on the night flight from New York. In a few minutes I am sitting across a cluttered Victorian desk from Dr. Foster. Dr. Belinsky sits in a large white corduroy wing chair near the desk, facing me.

Foster begins. "There is no question; it is Hays Syndrome," he says. "The residual mylotar test you had this morning confirms it unequivocally, Mr. Minton." He frowns slightly when he finishes speaking. This brings the black eyebrows close together, so that they form one long black line across his forehead.

Belinsky continues, "I believe that you know the prognosis." He waits for a moment, perhaps for a comment from me, and then he adds, "It is not good."

I find myself flushing a deep crimson. I realize that I should respond and I try to be as casual as possible in my tone. "Dr. Soames told me that I have ten to twelve weeks to live," I say, "and that there will be some deterioration." I find myself choking on these last words.

Both Belinsky and Foster look away, not wanting to share the embarrassment of my pain. "That's the general outline, yes," says Belinsky. "We've done many tests on you this morning. It will take several hours to get the results of the chemical tests and to fully analyze the residual mylotar test. I think we would do best to adjourn until tomorrow morning. Then, Mr. Minton, we can discuss possibilities further."

My back straightens. "Doctor," I say, "are you telling me that there is some hope?"

"Mr. Minton," Belinsky responds, "you have an incurable disease. To date the mortality rate from this disease has been one hundred percent. I don't want to hold out possibilities which aren't there. But I do want to analyze these tests, and I do want to talk to you again."

Foster adds, "What Dr. Belinsky is trying to say is that the picture does not look good, but we would like to exhaust every avenue. You know, if there wasn't hope our profession wouldn't exist."

But that does not, somehow, sound too hopeful.

VI

Oxford/July 9, 1978/3:00 P.M.

Good progress is being made on the con-
struction site on Banbury Road. The old row
houses have all been removed and digging has be-
gun for the foundations. This is going to be our
biggest project in England, a three acre enclosed
mall. The job foreman shows me around. He has
the pride of an old-fashioned craftsman, although
to date his job has been demolition.

"Let me show you some of the things we
dug up," he says, leading me to the small con-
struction shack. There I am treated to an interesting display of artifacts. The foreman has

become an archeologist and he tenderly protects each piece he displays.

"This mug is definitely from Beaumont Palace," he says. "That makes it 12th century and possibly used by Eleanor of Acquitaine or Richard the Lionhearted, who both lived at the Palace. The palace, of course, was directly over the site of the shopping center."

"Have you reported the finds to the authorities?" I ask, wondering about the legal status of the antiquities.

"Oh, yes, of course," says the foreman, patronizingly. "It's the law you know. All antiquities belong to the crown. I've already turned in some pieces, and expect to turn these in next week. We're still digging things up you know, every day. Here, I'll show you something we dug up just yesterday." With that he picks up a large black thing which looks a little like a soup tureen with strange, ugly designs around its outside.

"What is that?" I ask.

"Nice piece, isn't it?" he responds. Then he continues with the explanation, "It's what they call a 'Devil's Basin.' " Comes from the 17th or 18th century witchcraft cults. They used to wash in blood in them there basins before their prayers to Old Nick."

I suddenly find myself attracted to the piece. I hold it and it is warm to the touch. I think of the basin warmed by the blood of its users. My thoughts run on to witches and black magic. The foreman stares at me.

"Well, they certainly did strange things in the old days, didn't they," I say finally to break the silence.

"Don't you believe they're not doing those very same things right now, and right here in Oxford, too," he responds, without pause.

"You mean you think there is witchcraft here in Oxford?" I ask.

"I'm sure of it," he says.

"How do you know?" I want proof.

"I have my ways," says the old man. He will offer nothing more.

"Well, will they be angry that we've unearthed an old Devil's Basin?" I ask, trying to look at possible practical problems.

"They might be," he says, "but I'm trying to keep this one pretty quiet, get it over to the government office as soon as possible. No publicity, you know."

In the car on the way back to London, I pass through the old stone villages. I think about the morning meeting with Foster and Belinsky; Soames was right; the disease is incurable. Already the tingling is becoming more frequent and more painful. The reality of my own mortality begins to weigh on me. Passing an old Norman church reminds me of the immortality of the stones. There is a graveyard beside it. That reminds me, too. In three months I will be dead.

Then I think of the visit to Oxford. I try to think of the business details, but my mind keeps returning to the Devil's Basin. That foreman, he probably could put me in touch with a witch. All it would require would be three or four tankards of warm ale at one of the Oxford pubs. Then he'd spill whatever he knows.

Could witchcraft help? I wonder. If medicine fails, is it the only thing left?

VII

London/July 10, 1978/9:08 A.M.

It is one of those rare clear July days in London. There is warmth, summer, in the air. While we have our large English breakfast, I explain to Mary that I have an early appointment in Hanover Terrace, just across Regent's Park from the hotel. I suggest that she spend the day shopping again, and we agree to meet at the airport at six for the flight back to New York.

I walk slowly through the park, savoring the smells of an English summer, freshly mowed grass, recently watered trees, and the full perfume of the new roses. I listen to the nesting birds, and look up to catch a nuthatch on wing. As the path reaches the lake, I stop to watch and listen to children chasing the ducks. My left foot tingles. A cold fear grips my spine. I might see fall, but I won't make it to winter. No more winter. I shake my left foot; that relieves the tingling.

I am made to wait ten minutes in the outer office. The loss of time is more than I can bear. I am angry when I enter Dr. Foster's office, angry at the delay, angry at the injustice of having an incurable disease at forty.

Belinsky discourses again from the white wing chair. He holds a long curved pipe which he uses for emphasis. "Dr. Foster and I developed the residual mylotar test," he says. "The test shows the exact amount of damage done by the Hays Syndrome virus at any given point in time. It is able to pinpoint the course of the disease. You might say that it's rather like taking a photograph of the disease at any given time. All recorded cases of Hays have lasted between 80 and 86 days from onset." He wets his lips and puffs from the pipe, creating a haze of smoke between the two doctors and me. "On the basis of the residual mylotar," he says, "we can tell that yesterday was day fourteen for you."

The words are final, painfully final. I have listened carefully; I can do my arithmetic as quickly as the next fellow. "What you mean is that I have between 66 and 72 days left," I say to make sure that what I understand is the same as what I heard.

"I'm afraid that is right, Mr. Minton," says Foster. "As in your earlier diagnosis in New York, all of the other tests confirm and support the results of the residual mylotar test."

I feel a tingling pain in my right ankle. I want to shake the leg, but I don't want to draw their attention to it. I change my position in the chair and flex my right foot.

"We would like to treat you," continued Belinsky. "We have a number of therapeutic approaches that we have been experimenting with. One of them might prove successful." Belinksy seems to salivate at this last statement.

Foster adds, "Of course we'd keep you as comfortable as possible, and you'd have the satisfaction of knowing that you are contributing to the advancement of medicine."

I feel beads of perspiration on the back of my neck. The walls of the office seem to be closing on me. "Thank you, but I don't want to be a guinea pig," I say.

"Oh, there are no guinea pigs here," says Belinsky, rising, "Come, I give you a tour of the facilities."

Reluctantly, I accept the offer, and am briskly led upstairs by the doctor. He proudly points out the residual mylotar room, in the back of the first floor. "You have, of course, already seen that," he says with a chuckle. Then there are small examination rooms and modern labs also on this floor. The floor above has two operating theatres. Belinsky is a little vague about their use, and I get the impression that they may be used exclusively for autopsies. Above the operating rooms are two floors of patients' rooms, six to a floor. Each room is light and airy with good views of Regent's Park. Only three of the rooms are occupied. I cannot bring myself to speak to these patients; they are too frail and withered.

Back in Foster's office, Belinsky says, "You will stay, then, yes?"

"No, doctor, I said before, I don't want to be a guinea pig," I respond.

Foster looks at me and says, "You know it's so sad; we're very close to a breakthrough. You can't appreciate how close we are. I am sure that in another few months, maybe a year at the most, we'll have something. The sad part is the people who get it now; if only we could keep them going until we have the cure."

"Yours might be the breakthrough case," says Belinsky. "Stay with us. You've seen the facilities. If a cure is going to be discovered, we are the ones who are going to do it." Then he shrugs his shoulders and adds, "What have you got to lose?"

The ring finger on my right hand begins to tingle. I cover the hand, hoping to conceal it from the others. I look at Foster, saying, "I appreciate your interest, but look at it from my point of view. You've given me a death sentence. I'd like to enjoy the time remaining. I don't want to be an experimental animal in some laboratory."

The consultation is over. Belinsky escorts me to the door, reminding me that if I ever change my mind, I will be welcome at the clinic. As he speaks, I think of those frail, withered human beings whom I have just seen. I wonder if they have anything left to look forward to other than a daily visit to the torture chamber of the residual mylotar testing room. My feeling about doctors, that innate fear, has been confirmed.

VIII

Over the Atlantic/July 10, 1978/8:30 P.M.

"What's bothering you, Den? You're not yourself," says Mary. Cocktails are being served by the stewardesses, and Mary is right, I am distracted.

I have been quiet, painfully quiet, since we met at the airport. My mind has been going over options, options relating to Mary, options relating to myself.

When I don't respond, she continues, "C'mon you can tell me. What is it, some problem with the Oxford deal? The government giving you trouble?"

If only it were that simple, or that painless.

She has given me the opening. I may never have it again. And some day she's going to have to know, since I will soon be getting weak, maybe even unable to care for myself.

"Mary," I say, "something terrible has happened. I have an incurable disease, Hays Syndrome." Slowly I recount the story of the tingling pain, the visit to Dr. Soames, the diagnosis, the talk with Anderson, and finally the visit to Foster and Belinsky.

As I speak I watch Mary's face for a trace of emotion, but there is none. She puffs on her cigarette, and blows smoke between us. She seems to retreat into her seat, as if afraid that contamination may prove contagious. As I finish, I hear her say, "Oh my heavens! What will become of me?"

Of *her*! That's a bit much. She at least will live on. What will become of me, of me!!

I find myself angry that I have shared the news, annoyed at her reaction to it. There is no comfort, no warmth, no love.

As an afterthought she adds, "Den, we're too young for this sort of thing. There must be something, some way . . . "

I have no response. I turn back toward the window and take a fix on the starry night. We travel in silence for a few minutes, and then I hear her say, "Den, what are you going to do, about the office, about work?"

Always practical Mary. She wants to know if she is going to have to cope with an invalid at home for the next two and a half months. I respond, "I want to work. I want to keep working, and I don't want to tell anybody. I want to keep working as long as I can. And then, I don't know."

Suddenly there is a deafening ringing on the plane's public address system, followed by a voice. "This is your captain," says the voice. "There is no need for alarm. We have encountered mechanical difficulties with engine number two." The voice is frightened and it spreads fear among the passengers.

In a moment the plane banks sharply. Coats, blankets and briefcases rain down on passengers across the aisle. There is whimpering, cursing, a baby screams in the back of the plane. The lights flicker for a moment. There is an audible sigh when they return.

Then the captain comes back. "We will be making a special landing at Reykjavik Airport in Iceland, shortly. We are obtaining clearance for the landing at this time. Please keep your seat belts fastened and observe the 'No Smoking' sign." Again the words are reassuring, but the tone is frightened.

The stewardesses scurry to the far end of the plane, the safest part in case of crash. Their smiles are gone; they are no longer answering passengers' calls.

I find myself unconcerned, even hoping for a crash. It would be a swift end. It seems easier to deal with a fiery death now than the prospect of a slow and certain doom ten or twelve weeks hence.

Mary clutches my hand. "I'm scared," she

says. "I'm so scared." She lets go, then clutches at me again. "Oh, my God. Dennis, I'm scared." Her fingers press deeply against my knuckles, the nails breaking the skin. "I'm going to be sick," she says, grabbing an airsickness bag from the compartment in front of her.

I would like to comfort her. It seems the right thing to do. But I have no well spring of sympathy for her. I feel detached, distant. I think about her reaction when I told her about my Hays Syndrome. I measure it against her own hysteria in the face of potential death by fire. It tells me something, something I really don't need to know about the nature of my relationship with Mary, about Mary herself.

"We are descending to Reykjavik," comes the voice from the cockpit, "prepare for emergency landing." There are groans and shrieks, and the stewardess comes forward to demonstrate proper posture for the landing. We are doubled over in our seat when we feel the body of the plane touch ground. It wobbles along the runway several hundred feet. When it stops, the emergency chutes are opened and the plane is quickly emptied of passengers and crew.

While we wait at the airport for a backup plane, I learn that the "mechanical difficulties" the captain had referred to were two electrical fires of potentially disastrous dimensions. It was a very close call, indeed, but not close enough.

IX

New York/July 14, 1978/10:12 A.M.

Mary insists on coming to the office with me. She has spent the weekend treating me like an invalid. In spite of my protestations that I felt fine, she was constantly getting me cups of hot tea, covering me with an afghan to protect me from the chill of the air conditioning. It was silly, an expression of mock concern, all show and no reality.

She won't let me leave her sight. It's annoying, as if she has buried her real feelings beneath a guilt-produced layer of activity. She will play the good wife, however unlike her, and however nauseating to me it may be.

When we arrived at the office, a large pile of mail waits on my desk to be sorted. Mary helps, in her own useless way, picking at one piece at a time, asking a question about this matter, making a comment on that one. Halfway through the pile she picks up an invitation addressed to the two of us and opens it, saying, "Oh, a party; I do love a party."

She reads aloud, "Irene Minton requests the pleasure of your company at the marriage of her daughter, Barbara." She stops reading and asks, "Who is that, some cousin of yours, Den?"

I am concentrating on other matters. I ask Mary to read the name again. Then I realize, "That's Irene, my first wife," I say, "and Barbara was the child, our child. So she's getting married! Well, I'll be . . . "

Mary lights a cigarette. She seems uncomfortable to have reopened this piece of my past. She has known about Barbara and Irene, but they have not been subjects we have talked about for years. "Any regrets, Den?" she asks.

I try to summon my feelings and express them. "No," I say. "She doesn't mean anything to me, or I to her. That was all over so long ago. I wonder where they got our address from?"

Mary puffs on the cigarette. She doesn't seem convinced of my disclaimer of involvement. "Well, dear, do you want to go to the wedding?" she says.

I hesitate. The prospect of meeting my own daughter on her wedding day is an exciting one. But I also realize that she will be a total stranger.

The experience could be a terrible disappointment. "I don't think we should go," I say, "no point to it. I'm hardly the father-of-the-bride type, now am I, babe? But maybe we ought to send a gift."

"Yes," she says, "that's a good idea."

Mary continues picking at the envelopes. Each one she picks at requires a detailed explanation from me. I find I am spending more time giving Mary explanations than doing my own work. And the tone of her interest bothers me. It seems she has come to the office not to be at my side, but to learn the business, so that she can take over. That is too much.

"Mary," I say finally, "I'll make a deal with you. You go to Tiffany and buy a gift for that kid and I'll take you to lunch wherever you want."

She smiles. "Even the Maupassant?" she asks.

"Nothing's too good for you," I respond. A bargain has been struck. She goes.

I continue through the mail, sorting and dealing with things as I am able. The tingling begins again in my fingers; I shake my hand for relief.

One letter is a puzzle. The envelope, labelled *Confidential*, has a White Ridge, New York, postmark. Inside is a small card with the words, "We are aware of your problem. We can help. Call 914-884-2300. Ask for Tony."

I am intrigued. What problem could the card be referring to? Who would use such a strange secretive approach? Is it worth a telephone call?

Rereading the card carefully I think it must have been sent as a joke. I hesitate. I decide to call. For all I know, "Tony" might prove to be the source for a prospective deal.

I dial the number. Three rings, then a voice at the other end says, "Cryo Genius, Good Morning."

The name means nothing to me.

"May I speak to Tony, please," I say, following the instructions of the card.

There seems to be a disconnect, then after a while someone says, "Yeah, this is Tomasso. Who is talking?"

"Hello," I say, not sure I am speaking to the right person. "My name is Minton, Dennis Minton. I'd like to talk to Tony."

"Yeah, Minton. I'm Tony, Tony Tomasso," says the other. Then in a lower voice he adds, "You got my letter?"

It is no joke. The man at the other end of the phone has contacted me in a bizarre way for some unknown purpose. I am suddenly frightened. I want to bang the receiver down on the telephone and terminate this relationship. But I also want to find out what this man wants, what he is offering. So I keep talking. "Why did you write to me?" I ask.

"We want to help you, if you know what I mean,"comes the voice.

"No, I don't know," I respond. "What do you mean?"

"I don't like talking on the phone," says Tomasso. His voice is now impatient. "You come here," he says, "we can help you. We can help you better than Foster and Belinsky."

The names startle me. Tomasso knows more about me than I expected. He has now offered the key. The "problem" the card refers to must be my disease. The help? Well, Tomasso will explain in person.

"Where are you?" I ask.

Tomasso provides directions to White Ridge in The Catskills. He estimates the trip by car will take three hours. If I leave now I can be there by two. He promises to be waiting for my arrival.

As I leave the office, I leave a message for Mary cancelling our lunch date. Business, I say, has called me out of the city. *Business or death*, I think.

X

White Ridge/July 14, 1978/2:14 P.M.

The turnoff is barely noticeable, a small white sign "Cryo Genius" with an arrow, but Tomasso has warned me about it, and I don't miss it.

I turn right through the open iron gates. The place looks depressing. Beyond the small parking lot is a low concrete building. It might easily be a warehouse or a plant for light manufacturing. The absence of windows in the building is disturbing.

As I park, the twinges of pain in my left leg begin to hammer again. No good. I stagger on the way toward the side door marked ENTRANCE.

Inside I find myself in a short narrow hallway. In front of me is a locked door; over the door are two closed circuit television cameras and a device I recognize as a body sensor. All the latest equipment, and quite a lot of protection, unless they are sitting on a uranium mine here.

"Can I help you?" a disembodied voice inquires over the intercom.

"I'm Dennis Minton," I respond in a loud voice, hoping to be heard beyond the confines of this locked cubicle. "I have an appointment with Mr. Tomasso."

"One moment please," returns the disembodied voice.

In another moment a bear-like man opens the door in front of me and says, "Hello, I'm Tomasso. Follow me." He leads me through a glistening hallway to a small room. It is an office. But it is cramped and dark. Cheap panelling covers two walls, exposed cinderblock forms the wall covering for the others.

Tomasso indicates a chair for me and seats himself behind the desk. "So you need some help," he says. "That's good."

"What can you do for me?" I ask. I am studying the painting over Tomasso's desk. It is a garish Neapolitan scene, complete with a smoking Mt. Vesuvius in the background.

"We're aware of your problem and we'd like to help," he says.

"Problem? What problem? How help?" My eye settles on the gold brocaded drapes. They are not only tasteless, but also silly. There is no window behind them.

"Doctors," Tomasso says. I think he has

winked. "We keep in very close touch with doctors, referrals. In fact our organization was created to deal with problems like yours. You've got a disease. Maybe now it can't be cured. But maybe in six months or a year or a couple of years someone is going to find a cure which ain't going to do you any good unless you're still with us. That's where we come in."

"I still don't understand," I say. I am no longer considering the bad taste of the drapes or the grossness of the painting. My attention is fixed on this burly man with large, powerful hands.

"We put you on ice until the coast is clear," he says.

"On ice?" Could this be some sick joke?

"Yeah, on ice," he continues. "We freeze you; got all the equipment here. You get deep frozen and we keep you frozen until the disease is cured. Then you get thawed."

I don't believe it. "It doesn't seem possible," I say.

"Minton," Tomasso says, "there's a lot of things going on in this world you don't read about in the papers. We've done more freezing and thawing than you'd believe. It works, believe me, it works."

It is ridiculous. Yet Tomasso is serious, and I find myself drawn in, wanting to believe, wanting to accept any ray of hope. "But what's the proof? What's the proof that you can thaw someone?" I ask.

"Listen," he says, "We got your name,

didn't we? We know about your problem, don't we? We got a lot of connections in the right places, if you know what I mean. What more proof do you want?"

It isn't an answer. And yet Tomasso's refusal to offer proof is itself a form of proof. He is confident, so confident of himself no further proof is required. He is an old warlock, and I am about to wash my hands in the Devil's Basin.

"How much will it cost?" I ask.

"You're a rich man," he says. "You should not care about the money, if you can have your health. But now that you ask, I'll tell you. It's twenty grand for the job and the first year. After that there's yearly storage, four grand."

The price revives my doubts. I look around the windowless room, then at the burly Tomasso. None of it makes any sense. Finally, I say, "Is this some kind of sick joke?"

Tomasso looks serious. "It ain't no joke," he says. "We got thirty-four people in storage right now, and room for plenty more. You think about it. Seems to me you don't got too much to lose."

I get up to leave. There is a tingling pain in my left elbow.

Tomasso adds, "And if you don't want to use us, I wouldn't tell anybody about our little chat. You know what I mean?"

XI

New York Thruway/July 14, 1978/5:12 P.M.

I stop at a rest area on the Thruway on the way back. The tingling in my right foot has made driving difficult.

I call Mary. She is angry about the missed lunch.

"Aw c'mon, Mary, something important happened upstate, and I had to go up there. Look, I'm still stuck. You better have dinner without me. Maybe we can have that lunch at Maupassant tomorrow."

There is a grumble at the other end of the phone, and I know that she's not happy. Fences will have to be mended, but I'm not up to that sort of mending right now. Mary will have to wait.

Now I need quiet. I need to think. I eat alone, at a counter in the Thruway coffee shop. The sandwich is dry and tastes of plastic, a large icecube bobs in the glass of soda as I drink. The icecube reminds me; the clock behind the counter reminds me; the sealed plastic packet of mustard on the plate reminds me. I can't get away from Tomasso and Cryo Genius.

When I finish eating I sit in the parked car. In the silence I can think. Time seems suspended as I go over again and again all I know about Tomasso.

When I finally get back to the city it is nearly eight. I am tired: the tingling pains my left arm; but I have convinced myself that Tomasso offers a solution. I must talk to Anderson. I call him from a payphone.

"Sorry to bother you at home, Lee," I say.

"No bother," comes the reply. "I tried to reach you at the office this afternoon; they said you were out. How was England?" The voice sounded cheerful, but it is a contrived cheer, with a hollow ring.

"England?" I say. I have already put Foster and Belinsky out of my mind. "Oh, nothing new there, as expected." I pause. "Lee, could I see you, tonight? Something's come up."

"Come on over," responds Anderson. "No problem."

In the privacy of Anderson's book-lined library, I describe for him my visit to Cryo Genius

60

and the idea of being frozen to await a cure for Hays Syndrome. "Foster himself told me they are on the verge of discovery," I explain, "It may be only a year, maybe less. Then I'd be thawed and cured."

"What's the guarantee that these Cryo Genus people can freeze without killing you?" Lee asks.

"There's no guarantee," I say. "There's plenty of risk, I know that. But the other way, Lee, there's no risk, only death in ten weeks."

"How do you know these people are repuable, if I may apply that word to this sort of business?" asks Anderson the administrator.

"I don't know, Lee. I told you how Tomasso contacted me. He didn't offer any references. If you could check them out, that would be great. But, I'm not so sure a bad report would change my mind."

Anderson responds, "I'll see what I can do." Then he adds, "Dennis, there are legal problems here, too."

"I know," I say. "That's why I wanted to talk with you as soon as possible. I must have a new will. If I'm going to be frozen, I need to protect myself, so that when I'm thawed, my assets will be intact. Can you do it?"

"I think so," he says. "When do you want to be frozen?"

"As soon as possible," I answer. "By the end of the week, if I can. If I'm going to do it, I don't want to waste any time. Lee, I'm already starting to feel some deterioration setting in." There is a tremble in my voice. I shake my right arm twice, as if flicking water off it.

Anderson's eyes narrow. "Okay, Dennis," he says. "Let's go back to the office right now and I'll dictate the papers to the night staff. Then we'll have them all typed by the morning. It'll give us an extra business day before . . . " He hesitates, then he adds, "before you become unavailable."

XII

On the Road to White Ridge/July 18, 1978/ 1:35 P.M.

I find myself becoming uneasy as the car nears White Ridge. I try calming myself by reviewing the things that have been taken care of in a very few days, ticking them off on a mental list as proof that all is going smoothly. There was the will and trust and agreement. I didn't bother to digest their contents fully, but I can recollect the broad outline; my property is to be used to pay storage costs for my frozen body and to support Mary until I am thawed, then I am to resume control.

I remember that after the will and trust were

signed, Lee passed a number of other documents under my pen for signature. There had been corporate resolutions, dealing with the affairs of my many corporations, powers of attorney, giving Anderson authority to act for me, and letters resigning club memberships and cancelling all outstanding credit cards. These last I signed only reluctantly, arguing that I would soon be thawed and have to reapply. But Anderson had insisted, saying the resignations were essential for my protection.

I look out the car window and watch the trees pass quickly before my field of vision. I think of all the neat stacks of papers we left on Anderson's desk, all signed and ready to be distributed after my freezing is complete.

I think about Anderson's investigation of Tomasso and Cryo Genius. Tomasso, it turns out, has a criminal record. Cryo Genius is thought to be a front for the mob. That information should dissuade me, but it has had the reverse effect. I feel more confident that Tomasso really does mean business, and really can deliver a product that is so special it has completely shunned newspaper publicity.

And I think about Mary. Everything has happened so quickly, there has been so much to do, so many loose ends to tie up, I've never had that lunch at Maupassant, never confided to Mary about Cryo Genius or about being frozen. I could not bring myself to do it.

We have driven in silence for some minutes when I ask, "Lee, do you think I'm doing wrong by Mary? Do you think I should have told her?"

A space passes. Then Anderson says, "You had a tough choice. I suppose you could say this is like going on a business trip, a long business trip. You'll be back soon, six months, a year maybe. Meanwhile, you are trying to spare her the agony of separating."

He has spoken slowly, haltingly. And he doesn't sound convinced of what he has said. I conclude that Lee is not looking forward to the prospect of having to tell Mary himself. But tearful departures bother me; it's easier to do things this way. Anyway, Anderson is being well paid for his troubles.

The car reaches the iron gates and Anderson turns into the parking lot. As I get out, I rub my left arm, where the tingling has centered. I cross the lot, stopping near the door of the building to take two deep breaths of the summer country air. When will I smell fresh air again? With whose nose?

On his crowded desk, Tomasso clears a small space and spreads out the papers. Some require my signature, as principal; others need Anderson's signature as custodian. Some take both signatures.

The exchange of paper and money, back and forth, reminds me of the many real estate closings I've witnessed in Anderson's office. Here it is, a closing again, complete with certified check, as demanded by Tomasso for the cost of freezing and the first year's storage. The only thing missing is the real estate. But I realize that *I* am the real estate. I am the property being delivered by

Anderson to Tomasso. A knot forms in my stomach.

After all the documents are signed, piles of papers change hands and are put away in brief cases. Tomasso stuffs the certified check in his breast pocket. He says, "Well, you ready now?"

"I guess so," I say. My mouth is very dry; the words stick in my throat.

"Then you'd better say so long to your friend here; you ain't going to be seeing him for a while," says Tomasso, moving toward the door. He is anxious to get the job done quickly.

"I thought I might come along and watch the process, make sure everything goes properly," says Anderson, always trying to protect his client.

"Sorry," explains Tomasso, "but it's against the rules. Only authorized personnel are allowed in the freezing area. We got our secret processes we got to protect, if you know what I mean." He glares at Anderson.

"I see," says Anderson. "I wonder then if I'd be able to see Mr. Minton after the process is complete?"

"Oh, yes, that's alright," says Tomasso, sounding more friendly, "there's a viewing room, round the other side of my office. We'll bring Mr. Minton there so you can take a look, if you like, but it's going to take a couple of hours."

"I'll wait," he says. He wants to make sure that they really are capable of going through with the first phase of their program, the freezing.

Anderson promises me that he will make sure everything goes as planned. He says he intends to get weekly reports from Foster and Belinsky on the progress of the search for a cure for Hays Syndrome. As soon as a cure is found, he will instruct Tomasso to have me thawed.

"Is there anything else I can do, Dennis?" Anderson asks.

The knot in my stomach tightens. I want to ask Lee to help me escape. I am ready to turn and run, out of Tomasso's office, down the corridor and out to the parking lot. Only the dull twinges, shifting from my right leg to my left, and then reappearing in my right arm, keep me from running. I say, "No last requests. Only thanks again, baby, and I'm gonna see you again real soon."

I turn and follow Tomasso down the corridor and through the steel doors at the far end. Beyond the doors, Tomasso presses a button on the wall. The doors of an elevator open in front of us. The pain, the knot of fear in my stomach, gets worse.

The elevator is large. It reminds me of hospital elevators. The wide doors can easily accommodate a hospital bed. The control panel has several buttons, but none are labelled. I can judge only from the popping in my ears that we have travelled a considerable distance downward before the cars stops and the doors open.

In front of us is a hallway, its walls made from large white tiles. On the floor are smaller white tiles and overhead is a ceiling composed of white panels of light which seem to glow without a light source.

"This is quite a place you've got," I say.

"It's O.K." says Tomasso.

Twenty feet down the white hallway, Tomasso presses a button in the wall. A set of tiles moves into the ceiling, exposing a large tiled room.

"This is the preparation room," he says, "you get prepared here, before you go for your little swim." He laughs, adding, "I'll say so long now. Gertrude, the nurse, takes charge here. She will be here shortly. Meanwhile, you can get yourself undressed."

Tomasso leaves. I am alone in the preparation room. I study the table on one side of the room. It reminds me of a hospital stretcher. It is high off the ground, and has large wheels, but there is no mattress; instead the top of the table seems to be made of metal screening. Rather uncomfortable to lie on, I think. And then there is a strange undercarriage that looks like it could tip the whole table over at a ninety degree angle.

Suddenly a large woman of uncertain age enters the room. "I am Gertrude," she says. "You get undressed here. You put your clothes in plastic bag, here." She extends a hand holding a large plastic bag.

I am scared. I have a flash of insight. A Nazi guard is ordering me to leave my clothes in a neat pile, for later. I undress slowly, wanting to hold tight to my clothing. It is the last piece of humanity left to me.

Naked, shamed, my clothing in the bag, I watch while Gertrude seams it with an electronic device, printing my name and the date on the seam. I am impressed by the seaming device, by the efficiency. Surely they wouldn't go to such lengths about clothes if they don't think I'll be using them again.

"On the table," says Gertrude, "you get I.D. and then haircut."

I sit uncomfortably at the edge of the table. The nurse takes my right arm, roughly applying her electronic device to it, she gives me a painless tatoo, "DENNIS MINTON 071875."

Then the haircut. The prospect seems innocuous enough. Gertrude pulls an electric shaver from a recess in the wall. It whirrs loudly as she puts it to my neck. She reaches the top of my head and comes forward toward my face, cutting a broad path through my wavy brown hair. Before I can object, she has started again at my neck and is cutting another path. It is a scalping. In less than a minute, my entire scalp is bare. Then she whisks away my eyebrows and begins shaving my body.

I lay on my stomach while she shaves my back. Then I turn, and she completes the job, shaving legs, arms and torso. Her professionalism removes much of the discomfort. But when she is finished, I feel that more of my humanity is stripped away. I am grateful that there is no mirror in the room; I am spared the troublesome sight of myself hairless.

"Now, we begin," says Gertrude. I wonder what can come next.

"First you get paraffin spray," she says. "You will like that, but you must keep mouth and eyes closed."

I close my eyes. I listen to Gertrude's footsteps on the tile floor. Then I hear the swish of spray cans near my body and I feel something warm and sticky on my legs. The smell is unmistakably that of hot candles. I realize that I am being encased in wax, presumably as a prelude to some other process.

The paraffin spray seems to continue for some time. It is soothing, relaxing, not unlike a warm shower or the mist after a hot summer rain. At some point in the process, tubes, which feel like plastic drinking straws, are inserted in my nostrils, making breathing easier. The insertion has been explained by Gertrude, but her voice has been muffled by the wax which must now have covered my ears.

Shortly after the paraffin spray stops, I hear the muffled voice say, "Now you go in the bathtub. It's very cold there, so don't be surprised. You must hold your breath after the tubes come out. Then there will be no problems."

I hear steps on the tile. I have a dizzy sensation that the table has been wheeled around and around and then down some long distance. Suddenly I feel a cold blast of air in my nostrils. It is something so cold I am not sure I don't imagine it. The inside of my nose is seared and sore.

Then the air tubes are removed. I feel molten wax stuffed in my nose. I can't breathe, and I mustn't. I want to gag, but I can't.

I hold my breath and concentrate on sensation. I cannot see or smell, but I still have hearing, and I hear splashing. There is a liquid. The splashing grows closer. As it does, I find myself losing sensation. First my toes go, then my ankles, then up my legs to my waist. I lose my hands, arms, chest. Sensation stops at my neck.

I hear the liquid lapping at my head and I feel completely disembodied from the head down.

A curious sensation, I muse, as if I'd melted away.

A moment later, I feel nothing. I have been deep frozen in liquid nitrogen.

PART 2: THE TIP OF THE ICEBERG: 1978

I

Newtowne/July 28, 1978/4:40 P.M.

I feel waves of grogginess flow over me. I am waking, I suspect, from a deep sleep. With my eyes closed, in this state of semi-consciousness, I try to recall the time which has passed. I remember the sense of melting into a pool. Sensation ended abruptly with a light going out and darkness falling over my mind.

Then there is a dream. And I seek in the dream to find an answer. I dream of the Arctic. I am lying on an iceberg, arms and legs buried in snow. In the distance is a great white polar bear. The bear is coming toward me, slowly at first, then more quickly; finally he is running. Soon he is standing over me, his mouth wide open and his hot breath panting in my face. At that instant I feel fear and a terrible numbness from the cold and the lurching sense that I am asleep and dreaming and must awaken.

But in a moment the bear has disappeared. I am still lying on the iceberg, and the iceberg is sailing down a steaming jungle river, melting away into the mud. Again I feel fear. I am afraid that the floating iceberg will disintegrate and I will be left unprotected, to be eaten by the crocodiles approaching from either shore. Their teeth glisten in the moonlight.

Just as the iceberg starts breaking into small pieces, I hear a motor and the sound of voices, and I know that I am waking from a very deep sleep indeed.

For some block of time—how large I can't fathom—I lie at the edge of sleep, considering the polar bear and the new crocodiles and trying to make sense of them. Then the realities of my half sleep begin to stir in my mind.

I open an eye. It is a tremendous effort. The eye has been sealed closed, and I have to break the seal.

Vision is blurred, but in the blur I have the sense of a hospital room. There are two people huddled at the far end of the bed, whispering, and there is a blinding light overhead. Involuntarily I blink. The overhead light is too high in intensity for my vision. I close my eye more tightly. I want to retreat into the quiet place of sleep.

A sense of time is returning. I sense that

74

time measured in seconds or minutes, but not hours, has passed when I hear a voice, saying, "I'm very pleased to hear that, doctor. So you feel he'll be completely around fairly soon?"

There is some mumbled response, but I focus on the first voice, turning it over in my mind, breaking the words into small pieces. It is a voice I know, I have known it for a long time, I have heard it recently, or at least recently before the darkness of the pool.

I search for a name, and it comes. It is Anderson. Anderson, of course. How slow of me. I should have recognized him at once. Perhaps I'm under sedation.

The thought that Anderson is in the room, available to answer questions about time and place, to explain the things I don't yet understand, quickens my desire to rouse myself. I open my right eye again. It comes with more ease. After some blinking, I find I am better able to focus. Then, with difficulty, I break the seal on the left eye. I blink again; both eyes work. They work as a set. Together. Remarkable!

The light overhead is unbearable. I want to shield my eyes with a hand, but I can't remember how to command my hand to move. I'm not even sure that I have sensation in my hands. Instead, I blink and move my head slightly, taking my eyes out of the direct rays of the intense light.

Lying with my eyes open, I become aware of the white bedsheets, the beige walls and the overhead television set. Clearly this is a hospital and I am here for a reason, which I cannot quite remember, though I think it has something to do with that pool and the darkness.

Then I feel pain in my right arm. It is the first sensation there, and, in one way, a relief. I see the intravenous tubing and a needle imbedded in the vein at the elbow joint. That explains the pain.

But then I have a similar pain in my left arm. I look and find no intravenous in that arm. I stare at the arm. The pain is a tingling and a twinge. It is familiar. It reminds me. It opens up a floodgate of remembrances. Hays Syndrome, I have Hays Syndrome. That's what's producing that pain.

And then I remember further. I remember Tomasso and Cryo Genius, and I realize that the disease must be cured. That's why I've been thawed. That's why I'm in a hospital.

I am excited by the prospect. The excitement rouses me further. I find a voice and call out from the bed, "Lee, Lee Anderson, is that you?"

From the far end of the bed one of the figures approaches me. He leans over the bed. The overhead light is behind him and makes visual recognition impossible, but I hear, "Yes, Dennis, I'm here." It is indeed Anderson.

I am elated, but I want a full explanation. "Where am I? How much time has passed?"

There is a long pause before I get an answer. Then Anderson says, "This is Newtowne General Hospital."

He seems to be waiting for a reaction, or a sign of recognition. I digest that information. I am in a hospital. I had concluded that just by looking around. But it is "Newtowne General Hospital". And Anderson sounds uneasy as he says it.

I consider the name of the place. *Newtowne.* I have never heard of it, have no recollection of it. My mind flashes with possibilities. Can it be, I wonder, that such an abyss of time has passed since my freezing that cities have fallen and new cities have been built? Could my sleep have been measured in terms of years, perhaps even decades? The thought is chilling. I hadn't planned to sleep for years.

I am anxious. "Where is this hospital, and when?" I ask, "especially when, Lee?" I plead for an explanation.

"The hospital is in Newtowne," says Anderson, still speaking slowly and leaning over the bed. "It's the county seat of Amesfort County, New York, not too far from the Cryo Genius place in White Ridge." At the reference to Cryo Genius, Anderson lowers his voice, as if afraid he might strike an exposed nerve.

But mention of Cryo Genius does not disturb me. I have already recollected the visit to Cryo Genius and the fact that I had gone there to be frozen to await the cure for Hays Syndrome. I am interested only in finding out how much time has passed and whether I have already received the cure.

"When is it?" I ask. "How much time has passed since the freezing?"

I watch Anderson walk to the foot of the

bed. He whispers something to the white-coated man standing there. Then he returns closer to me again, and says, "Not much time has passed, Dennis. In fact you were frozen only ten days ago!"

I am startled. I have braced myself to be told of a sleep measuring years. A ten day freezing is an anti-climax. Still, if the cure has been found, if it has been administered already, that is all that is important.

Anderson is standing at the side of the bed now. I can see his light gray pinstripe suit. His features haven't changed at all. Of course, he hasn't changed because only ten days have passed since the freezing, but at least that damn disease has been cured.

Then I speak to him. "The cure, what about the cure for Hays Syndrome? Have I had it yet?"

He looks at me, but he doesn't speak. I see him gesture to the white-coated man. The man comes forward and the two of them seems to confer in low whispers for an inordinate length of time.

Anderson speaks even more slowly than before. He is choosing each word as if he were picking pearls for a matched necklace. "I'm afraid we have some bad news for you, Dennis," he says, "Hays Syndrome hasn't been cured yet. You were not thawed because a cure had been found for Hays Syndrome."

I don't have time to fully grasp what Anderson has said. There is the sharp jab of a hypodermic in my left arm, and I sense sleep overtaking me once more. This time it is a fitful sleep, filled with dreams of a baking sun on the Sahara.

II

Newtowne/July 29, 1978/2:12 P.M.

When I awake again, the intense overhead light is gone. My eyes fall on an array of bright floral arrangements across the room from the bed. I scan a dozen bouquets and plants and my mind flickers with the thought, Am I dead? Is this a funeral chapel? But the thought passes; I sense the hospital room and I hear the dim drip of the intravenous.

There are two figures standing near the left side of the bed, a tall man and a short woman. Looking at the man summons my most recent moments of consciousness. The man is Anderson, I remember, and I remember also that Anderson has explained that I am in a hospital and only a few days have passed since the freezing at Cryo Genius.

Then I look at the woman. I try to focus on recollections dealing with her. She looks familiar. Her body is wrapped in a tight-fitting sweater and skirt; the outlines of that form bring remembrance. It is Mary. I am upset by her presence. There are explanations owed, a debt I wish to forget.

I close my eyes for a long time. Perhaps they will go away. But when I reopen them, the two figures are still there, whispering. I know I will have to deal with them.

"Mary, Mary," I call weakly, "I want to talk to you." I feel clear-headed, but as I listen my words have a dull echo. It must be the sedation.

At my call, the two figures come closer to the bed. Mary puts one hand to my head and pats it softly. "I really should be angry with you, Den," she says, "going off like that. Not even leaving me money for lunch at Maupassant."

It is said in jest, but so are the most truthful thoughts, always. Mary's primary concern through this ordeal, through my freezing and thawing, has been her lunch, her confounded lunch at Maupassant.

Her words anger me. Then I focus on the strange feeling on my head. Mary is patting, rhythmically, but there is no hair. The pats daub at my mind, reminding me of Gertrude and the sheep shearing. I am bald, hairless and shamed. I want to close my eyes and be alone. I want that confounded patting to stop. But it continues, and I must respond.

"I'm sorry," I say, looking at her, "sorry I didn't tell you. I thought it would be easier that way, thought you'd worry less."

She says, "You certainly look silly without any hair, Den." She continues to pat my baldness, to keep reminding me of my shame. I close my eyes. The rhythm reminds me of waves beating against the beach, a distant beach I once knew and shared with another woman. But there are no sand dunes here, no ocean breeze, only my wife and my lawyer and this hospital room.

"Mary, cut the tom tom," I say, finally in frustration, "you're giving me a headache."

"Sorry, Den," she says and she stops, retiring to the window to light a cigarette.

I turn toward Anderson. Mary's massage has fully awakened me. I want an explanation. "What is going on here, Lee," I say. "Why am I here?"

Anderson hovers over the bed, near my elbow. "Dennis," he says, "There's been a problem."

"What? What is it?" I am frustrated, exasperated. I want to know what I am doing in this hospital bed and no one is giving me the answer.

Anderson looks at Mary and then at me. He bends his shoulders over the bed and speaks softly. "Cryo Genius was raided by the authorities, three days after you were frozen. You're very lucky to be here at all." He pauses and I nod to indicate that I understand what has been said.

Then Anderson continues, "Yes, you're very

81

lucky indeed. Our suspicions were right. The place was being used by the mob, but the use they had for it was disposal of unwanted enemies. You might say that was their wholesale business. They would murder and freeze those marked for execution. It's sort of a switch on the old blocks of cement trick."

I nod again. I am understanding, but a little dimly.

"The F.B.I. was maintaining surveillance on the place," continues Anderson. He is warming to the story. "They got a good tip that the remains of a particular underworld character, Frenchy Lavalle, could be found at Cryo Genius. Somehow, Tomasso and his people became aware that the F.B.I. was going to raid. They fled, and haven't been heard from since. Meanwhile the F.B.I. found thirty-five frozen individuals in the Cryo Genius vaults. It was with some difficulty that the doctors figured out how to work the thawing mechanism. The first ten cases thawed had all been pre-murdered gangland style. Apparently those bodies all came from one particular section of the freezing room."

Anderson pauses as if to catch his breath, then he continues, "You were the next one thawed. They did that yesterday morning, and you've come around very well indeed. The doctors are quite pleased. But last night the freezing mechanism failed. All of the others are lost."

Again he pauses, but only for an instant. He does not wait for me to nod understanding. He adds, "You are the only survivor."

I close my eyes again. I have heard enough. I need sleep, sleep to filter and percolate my thoughts. By an act of will, in a moment Anderson and Mary are gone and I am alone, with sleep.

During the last two days, Mary had been cheerful, constantly solicitous, overly solicitous, just as she had been those few days in New York.

III

Newtowne/August 8, 1978/4:20 P.M.

"You look cute with short hair, Den," she says.

I smile, but there is no depth to it. The tingling in my right leg has become acute. It isn't a peripheral sensation any more; now it is real pain, pain constantly reminding me of my disease, and the prognosis, and there is nothing to smile about.

During the last two days, Mary has been cheerful, constantly solicitous, overly solicitous, just as she had been those few days in New York. She comes to the hospital early every morning and she stays late. She hovers over me. The cheer and the hovering are really too much.

"Thanks, baby," I say, to maintain the facade. But I feel awkward. My closely-shaven head, now grown into a short crew cut, that reminder of my visit to Cryo Genius, of my hope destroyed, embarrasses me.

"Maybe you should keep it that length, all the time," she adds.

How damned insensitive can she be? Bad enough to be reminding me of my hair, now she is also reminding me of the shortness of time I have left. I refuse to respond. Instead, I close my eyes and lay back on the hospital bed.

There is a long silence, then Mary raises another subject. "Lee tells me they're going to let you out of the hospital tomorrow, dear," she says.

"Yes," I say, looking up from the bed, "But I'm afraid that young County Prosecutor, Mr. Dwyer, has his own plans for me tomorrow, too."

Mary lights a cigarette. She sits on the edge of the armchair. The smoke tingles in my lungs and I face away from her. "You mean the grand jury?" she says.

I nod. There is a sharp tingling pain in my left arm. I flinch and look back to see if Mary has noticed. She is puffing on her cigarette and gives no reaction.

"I don't understand why they want you to testify before the grand jury," she continues. "What do you know about Cryo Genius? Anyway, they still haven't even found that Mr. Tomasso."

I clench the knuckles of my left hand. It

eases the pain and stifles the frustration. Mary's question again reminds me of my fragile mortality, and I'm not going to let the reminder pass this time.

"Listen, kid," I say, "They want my testimony 'cause I'm the only honest person who saw the inside of Cryo Genius in operation. I'm the only honest person who can explain it all, right from the little *Confidential* envelope to the final dunking by Frau Gertrude. I was there." My voice is rising. I am no longer speaking, I am screaming, the words coming out like cannonfire. "And they want my testimony now, before the grand jury, because I'm not going to be around when they find Tomasso. I'm going to be gone, DEAD, SIX FEET UNDER!!!"

"Dennis, don't talk like that, calm yourself," she yells. "Nurse, nurse, come quickly. He's hysterical, violent."

In the interchange she has averted my gaze. Afraid to look into the eyes of a corpse, I think, and so I close them.

IV

Newtowne/September 3, 1978/8:12 A.M.

I stand on the terrace of our motel room. I breathe in the fresh morning air. It is cold, suggesting cold days and months to come. In the clear early light, the green hills are splashed with sun. There are dots of yellow and red, maples and oaks turning early to fall foliage. The first of the season. The autumn feeling of the morning frightens me. It tells of time, and for me, time means death.

As I stand on the terrace, I give my right arm an unconscious shake. It relieves the pain. I wonder how much longer a shake will be able to do it. I wonder how much longer I'll be able to walk.

I see it all as a race, the tortoise and the hare, my life and Tomasso's trial. Tomasso, the fugitive, has finally been found, and the trial is to begin today. I doubt that I'll still be around when it is over, particularly with the production I see this young prosecutor, Dwyer, is working over. He has connected into *Time* magazine and national television coverage, billing the murder-freezings as the "crime of the century." There is no doubt that Mr. Dwyer is trying to build the case out of all proportion, and may make it run on for months, all to enhance his own fortunes.

Now I wait, wait for Mary to finish those things that women do which take ever so long before they can face the world in the morning. And then we will have breakfast in the motel coffeeshop and walk the few blocks to the courthouse, to arrive before the festivities begin.

While I wait I chew one of the tablets. That relieves the pain. I close my eyes and inhale the fresh air again. I hear the chirping of some early migrating birds. I once loved birds, but that was some long time ago. I can't quite remember when.

Mary shouts from the room, "There's a call for you, Den."

I open my eyes, draw one more breath of fresh air and return to the room, picking up the phone with a "Hello!" There is a woman's voice, heavily accented, saying "Vee are aware of your problem. We can help." I recognize the words immediately. It is the Cryo Genius trademark. And the voice, that voice is familiar too.

She does not wait for an answer, but continues, "Come to Louie's Diner, on South Forest, in five minutes." Before I can respond, the telephone has clicked off.

I don't find myself weighing possibilities. There is no decision to make. I have made it reflexively. I merely call to Mary, in the bathroom, "Something's come up. You go and have breakfast. I'll meet you at the courthouse."

"What's the matter?" comes her voice, more in curiosity than concern.

"Nothing, nothing at all," I say. "See you later." I slam the door, walk down the corridor and out the side door of the motel. It's as simple as that. That's all there is to it.

As I walk up Forest Avenue the four blocks to Louie's Diner, I have to stop twice because of the discomfort, the pain and the tingling. I rub my leg, and there are doubts. Am I walking into a trap, an ambush? But there is also excitement. Tomasso and Gertrude saved me once. They can do it again. They have a way.

When I get to the diner, I hesitate as I open the door. A woman in a booth in the back motions toward me. It is Gertrude, and I am not surprised. A man is cramped into the booth with her. His heavy hands and deep set eyes remind me of Tomasso, but the blond hair and the full beard obscuring the face make identification impossible.

The man speaks first. "We want to help you," he says, looking directly at me. "We know about your disease. We know you ain't got much more time to live. We thought you might be interested in finding another place where they do a

91

little freezing, if you know what I mean."

The voice is unmistakable. "Tomasso?" I say, "How did you get out of jail? What's going on here? You're expected on trial this morning."

"No questions now," the other says. "We don't got no time, understand?" Tomasso is serious. This is no game. Tomasso and Gertrude are fugitives, about to flee the jurisdiction. Unlikely as it may seem, they have stopped long enough to give me an opportunity to join them.

In spite of the injunction, I ask, "Where is this new place?"

"It ain't around here," says Tomasso. He pauses, then adds, in a low voice, "It's in Canada, someplace where there ain't no cops."

"We are going now," explains Gertrude. "We thought to offer you should come too, if you vant."

"You're going to be frozen?" I ask Tomasso. I can't believe that he is going to submit himself to the process.

He nods. "Thought I'd do it till things cool down, understand?"

"How you getting there?" I ask.

"We've got a car here, one of our cars," says Tomasso, cocking his head and gesturing toward the window of the diner. He may have winked. "We drive part of the way and fly part of the way," he continues, "But that's enough questions: we want to get going, so we're a long way from here by the time the court starts at ten o'clock."

I look at the two of them and I am frightened. The pain in my left arm makes me squirm. I hesitate, then say, "I don't have much choice. If I don't go, I'm dead by the end of the month. If I do go, at least I have a chance." Then I add, "But why should you people be so generous with me? I don't get the angle."

"C'mon," says Tomasso, "we'll have plenty of time to talk about that." And Tomasso eases his large body out of the booth. As he turns to leave he lets a crisp twenty flutter to the table.

We walk to the car. My mind fills again with thoughts of kidnapping and entrapment. I want to know how Anderson will know of my whereabouts. They assure me that Anderson will be notified as soon as the escape is successfully completed.

We squeeze into the front seat of the large brown Cadillac. Tomasso and Gertrude sandwich me in the middle. Tomasso swerves out of the lot and roars down the road, breaking the speed limit by at least twenty miles. I am frightened and uncomfortable and hoping. And the hell with Mary.

Gertrude is friendly, too, for a Nazi. In an hour I
am on a first name basis with them. Tobiasso has
a penchant for distressingly high speeds, but the

V

Montreal/September 3, 1978/12:14 P.M.

I am starting to have regrets and doubts. A-
gain I have left Mary without explanation; again I
am leaving the whole burden of responsibility on
Lee Anderson; again I have opted for a path of
uncertainties.

The trip from Newtowne to Montreal has
been easy. Tomasso has proven, surprisingly, to
be a nice guy, a regular guy, and an easy talker.
Gertrude is friendly, too, for a Nazi. In an hour I
am on a first name basis with them. Tomasso has
a penchant for distressingly high speeds, but the
Cadillac seems able to absorb them.

The only really apprehensive moment comes

crossing the border. But Tomasso's gamble that we are crossing before the disappearance is noticed proves correct.

At the private aircraft hanger of the Montreal airport, I stretch my legs for the first time since the start of the journey. My right leg pains and tingles. I check my supply of painkillers. Only eight left. I wonder how I'll be able to deal with that pain without those little tablets. We better get to this new freezing place soon. I frown and chew one of the tablets.

"You hurt?" asks Gertrude. She has been watching me.

"I'm having some pain. I'll be all right," I answer.

She winks. "Soon now, very soon," she says.

Tomasso directs us to an old four-seater Cessna. The plane looks ancient and in poor repair. I think of the near crash on the way home from London. I think too of the irony of going down in the Canadian arctic. It seems so unfair. I have tried so hard to beat this thing, this Hays Syndrome. And every effort has seemed to turn to dust and ashes.

We climb aboard the plane. My anxieties about the flight are increased when I meet the pilot, who doesn't seem able to speak English fluently. He also trembles slightly. "Don't worry," says Tomasso, "Ference was the best pilot in the Hungarian Air Force before he came to work for us."

I tense again as we rattle along the runway

for takeoff. It doesn't seem possible that this tin can will ever be airborne. Then, just as I have despaired, and I am expecting a fiery end in the evergreens at the end of the runway, I feel the ride become smooth and the plane rises slowly over the field. I watch carefully through the porthole. As the plane rises higher, my tension begins to dissipate and I enjoy the vistas below. The urban environment quickly yields to residential areas and suburbia, and that soon yields to the forests and the mountains.

"How far are we going?" I call to Tomasso, over the noise of the engine.

"You'll see! You'll see!"

I watch more closely, trying to judge distance and direction from the position of the sun and visible landmarks. But it is three hours before a great body of water spreads out in front of us on our left. My observations suggest it must be Hudson's Bay. The plane starts to lose altitude, and we land at Richmond Gulf, a small town on the shore of the Bay. Then to an old Ford station wagon for the last leg of the trip, over dirt roads to Chadworth.

I find myself becoming depressed again. The trip seems so long. I'm in an unfamiliar place, a strange and rugged terrain. And here I am between two people whom I know to be murderers and fugitives from justice. I don't have any control, not even the semblance of control over this environment. I'm scared.

The trip to Chadworth takes two hours. It isn't very nice. The road is rough. In many places there is only one lane, with sidings to permit on-coming vehicles to pass. Fortunately there is little traffic. On both sides of the road there are thick forests of pine, almost obscuring the late afternoon sunlight.

"This is Chadworth," says Tomasso, finally. "Go to it, Gertrude."

I look around and see only a widened two lane road, a small post-office-cum-general-store and two shacks. I am about to ask Tony about the local populace, when I feel a sudden blow on the back of the head. It comes from my right, from Gertrude, and I can even hear her mutter "Sorry" as I slip into unconsciousness.

VI

Chadworth/September 3, 1978/6:25 P.M.

My head has a large bump, and it hurts. And I am angry, to be betrayed by my new friends at the very end of our long trip together. I can't understand it.

I am awake immediately, and asking questions. "What's the point of hitting me over the head? What did you people gain by doing that?"

"Sorry," says Tomasso. "It's local rules here. The patient isn't supposed to see the outside of the building. That way you can't ever identify it, because you ain't never seen it, if you know what I mean."

"It was only a light bang," says Gertrude.

"Here I give it alcohol massage. It will go away." With that she applies some alcohol to a sponge and gently strokes the bump. Her technique is excellent; very soothing.

I am sitting on a nondescript couch in what I assume is a sitting room of this new freezing facility. It seems seedier than Cryo Genius. But that is only a feeling, an osmosis of something.

A short man with thick white hair enters. "This is Mr. Smedly," says Tomasso, introducing us, "Mr. Wharton Smedly."

"I'm sure you'd like a little visit about, Mr. Minton, before you start your formal holiday with us," says Smedly in the clipped accents of one who has studied long and hard to be British. Too cheerful, I think, too cheerful. Instead of easing my fears, this confounded cheeriness heightens them. Still, I agree to the tour, and take some reassurance from Smedly's openness.

First we go to the preparation room. Smedly leads the way, I follow close after him, with Gertrude behind me, and Tomasso trailing at the end. He is really not that interested in the tour. Seen one freezing facility, you've seen them all, I guess.

This preparation room is much smaller than the white tiled room I remember from Cryo Genius. No, this one is the size of a cramped doctor's examining room. It has a vintage model electric razor hanging on the wall. "How would you like to do your sheep shearing with that old thing, Gertrude?" I ask. She laughs.

Smedly explains that the paraffin treatment is administered through old DDT spray guns. It certainly seems a low budget operation. Everything is ancient, or second hand, here.

From the preparation room we go to the freezing room itself, a small interior space with a large aluminum vat which resembles nothing so much as an oversized bathtub. The size and shape of the vat summons the dim recollection of Cryo Genius, of feeling myself melting away into a distant pool. I turn to Gertrude and say, "It was different at Cryo Genius, wasn't it? Wasn't it?"

Tomasso answers. "Yeah," he says. "We did things a little fancier. We had a big pool, eight foot deep, used to lower the guys into it. Worked like a charm. But it ain't gonna matter whether you get lowered into a pool or dropped in this here bath. It's all the same."

Tomasso's comments make me think of something else. The vat is empty. Where is the liquid, the liquid nitrogen needed to effect the freezing. I say to Smedly, "How come the vat is empty?"

"Well, there you have a good question, a very good question, old chap," he responds. "I'm afraid our last shipment of liquid nitrogen has evaporated. You know it will only last so long. We are waiting for a shipment, expect it any day, you know."

I begin to feel a quickening in my pulse. I have been brought to this uninhabited wasteland with the promise of being frozen, and now the promise is evaporating, too. And the man who is telling me about it has the cheerfulness of a low grade moron. I am angry. "You mean to tell me,

I've come all this way and you don't have the ability to freeze me?" My voice bounces off the aluminum vat and echoes back in my ears.

"Not today, old chap, maybe tomorrow," says Smedly. "I'm sure we'll be able to do it by the time we get payment from your lawyer in New York." Smedly's right eyebrow raises slightly, as if to emphasize the reference to payment.

I catch the words and the gesture. I understand. Pain grips my right arm. "How much money?" I ask.

"Thirty-five thousand dollars," says Smedly cheerfully, adding a detailed list of services provided. "That covers freezing, one year's storage and guaranteed thawing at such time as your agent may designate. Storage after the first year is on an annual contract basis. Five thousand a year."

"That's a lot of money," I say. My anger is growing. "Things were cheaper at Cryo Genius, and their equipment was a lot better than yours."

Smedly leans against the wall. "This is a dangerous business," he says. "You might say that our overhead is pretty high, old boy." He laughs; Tomasso laughs; Gertrude smiles.

"What about Tony and Gertrude?" I ask. "Are you going to wait to freeze them until my money comes through?"

Smedly grunts something, but Tomasso interrupts, "You see, Dennis, Smedly here is all alone. We thought it would be better for all concerned if we didn't get no freezing job on us until you get taken care of."

"You and Gertrude are Smedly's body-guards, then, is that it?" I ask accusingly.

"We are and we ain't," says Tony. "Listen, we all need Smedly to do the job and do it right. Gertrude and me is going to get frozen, just like you, but Smedly would rather not be all alone with you. So, we'll wait to get frozen, until he's got your money."

I catch Tony's glance as he speaks. I feel affection for him. We have shared experiences, and the sharing has made me respect this strange, burly fellow. I see him as basically good natured, and I try to appeal to that nature. "Tony," I say, "You know I'm sick. Time is crucial. Every day I get worse. I can't wait."

"I know. I know what you mean," says Tomasso. He is a well spring of compassion. Then he adds, "I'm sorry, Dennis, but that's the way it's gonna be. Ain't nothing we can do about it."

Smedly adds, in a tone that sounds concerned, "See here, you can call your lawyer's office right now. We have a telephone line open to New York. You can tell him that you are safe, but of course not where you are. Tell him he'll be getting an invoice from the Hudson Bay Frozen Fish Company in a day or two. It'll be for fish, frozen fish, thirty-five thousand dollars worth of frozen sole. You just tell him it's okay to pay that invoice, and that he'll be getting more information later."

Smedly looks to Tomasso and then he continues, "We all understand, old chap, about your problem and the time factor. As soon as your

103

lawyer wires us the money, I'm sure we'll have no trouble with our liquid nitrogen delivery, and then the job can be done in no time at all."

I look from Tomasso to Smedly to Gertrude and back again to Tomasso. The tingle in my right shoulder has become a dull pain. I rub it. Shifting my glance from one to the other of these people, I feel trapped. It has been a wild goose chase. I have followed Tomasso to the frozen north only to be held up for a ransom of thirty-five thousand dollars. And now my very life depends on the speed with which Anderson dispatches the money.

I am alone. I am frightened. I am cold. Finally, I say, "Where's the telephone?"

VII

Chadworth/September 7, 1978/3:10 P.M.

Gertrude calls me. "It is that lawyer friend of yours, on the phone, again."

I rush to Smedly's office and the two piece standup telephone with the open wire to New York. For Anderson it's a cheap call, he dials a local New York number and gets to speak to an unidentified part of Canada.

"Hello, Lee," I say in excitement, only to be splashed with the cold water of the secretarial, "One moment for Mr. Anderson, please."

And then he is on. And I am filled with questions. Questions about whether he has reconsidered, whether he has any doubts he wants to share, whether he has word that Hays Syndrome has been cured.

I begin by saying, "The money arrived this morning. Thanks for the speed."

"And when is Hudson Bay going to freeze the sole?" comes the question from New York.

"They're filling the liquid nitrogen vat right now," I say. "Should be in an hour or two, three at the most. You don't have any second thoughts, Lee, now do you, any doubts?"

"No, this seems the only alternative right now," he says. "By the way, you might be interested to know that you're in hot water over the Tomasso trial, so it is perhaps just as well that you disappear for a while."

"What do you mean?" I don't understand how I can be in hot water. I was only a witness.

"Well," says Anderson, "you were a witness, and you were subpoenaed, and your failure to report on the morning the trial opens is a technical contempt of court, a mere technicality, of course. Still, I don't mind if you are going to be beyond the reach of the process server for a while."

Gertrude comes in. She gestures that the vat is almost ready. It is time to start preparations for the freezing.

"Listen, Lee," I say. "Can't talk any longer. They say it's time I get ready for the freezing. Wish me luck, baby."

"Good luck," says Anderson. "Don't catch cold."

"Thanks, Lee, thanks. See you soon." And I hang up.

When the receiver is back on the hook, I realize that I haven't asked him about Mary or her reaction. I guess I don't really care.

I undress and place my clothing in a small pile in the plastic bag. I think of Mary. That business will all have to resolve itself when I am thawed. First thing.

I've seen/white like this before, out in the fog
of my mind. I can't remember when or how.
All I know is that it has to do with the cold.
I bundle the overcoat closer. The cold

PART 3: ICE COLD: 2008

I

Chadworth/February 15, 2008/10:15 A.M.

I am startled by the light. I am confused,
weak in the knees and in the head. That light,
that bright, white light, nearly blinds me as I
walk out of the door of the building.

There is white as far as I can see, in all directions. A glistening unrelieved white. No hor-
izon. It makes me cover my eyes with a hand.
I've seen white like this before, but in the fog
of my mind. I can't remember when or how.
All I know is that it has to do with the cold.

I bundle the overcoat closer. The cold
wind catches on my bald head; and I think of
the three toes on my left foot. The toes that

aren't there.

John, the attendant, comes out behind me. "Cold enough for you out there, Mr. Minton?" he asks, stepping through the whiteness.

"Yes, yes, it is cold," I respond. As I speak I hear the echo of a distant voice speaking haltingly, and it is my voice. It seems to take me too long to frame words; speaking is an effort. I can't seem to speak fluently.

I can think back, reconstruct all the things I've said since waking. It's all been responses to questions, a nod, or a "yes" or "no." Nothing more complicated. I have asked nothing; I haven't felt the capacity to ask, and yet I have questions.

I don't recognize this place. I can't remember how I got here, or why. The whiteness and the cold are foreign. I have the uncertain sense that I am lost.

Three toes are gone. I know that. While I was still in bed John told me, or at least asked if I knew the toes were missing. The question alarmed me. I touched my foot and found the three middle toes gone. That disturbed me even more. Three toes are gone. Surely that's a thread I can seize on and follow back to some further source.

I concentrate on the missing toes, on the feeling in my shoe that they are still there and in pain. Suddenly there is a deafening noise behind me and to the right. I turn. And as I do so, John yells, "Stand back, Mr. Minton, it's the amfocrapht."

I take two steps back toward the safety of the building. The noise grows louder, then it

110

changes key and becomes a whir. Out of the white appears a large red device.

For a moment it hovers ten feet above us, a flying saucer with a shiny red exterior. I am frightened: I've never seen anything like this before. Only an act of will controls my fear. Then my mind clicks more quickly. I realize that John has identified the thing, even given it a name. For John this sort of thing must be commonplace. I must have forgotten something. My memory must need a jog.

With a sigh, the thing descends to the ground. Clouds of white crystals are blown up as it settles in place. The clouds remind me again of this white substance, but still it has no name.

As it sits in front of me, not more than twenty feet away, I try to assess the red device. It looks less than twenty feet long, but not much less, and six or seven feet high. Its width is about the same as its height. Curiously, it seems to be completely without windows. Sitting noiselessly in front of me, the amfocrapht looks like nothing other than a great red cigar.

Then there is the whir of a small motor. A square of the red metal folds down onto the ground, providing steps. A man scurries down the steps. He is wearing a one piece blue jumpsuit. It covers all extremities and runs up to his neck. It is unlike any garment I have ever seen.

The man's outfit, his very demeanor, frightens me. But he greets John, they seem to know each other, and seem relaxed in talking together. I only know John since waking, but I count

111

him a friend. If this man in blue is John's friend, perhaps I shouldn't be so suspicious.

Behind the man is a woman. Her jumpsuit is virtually a duplicate of the one the man wears. It too covers all extremities and runs up to the neck. It, too, has a diagonal row of snaps. The only difference is in color. The woman's suit is gold, and has a narrow green design on each wrist.

The woman comes directly to me. She smiles and says, "Hello, Mr. Minton. I'm Janet Helson."

I'm confused. The smile is ingratiating, warm and open. It stirs a memory of something long past, but a deep English fog still seems to cover my mind. I don't recognize her. I've never seen her before, that I can recall. Yet she knows very well who I am. I try to focus on the name. I search my recollections. I can't think of ever knowing anyone named Helson. And the name, Janet, that too means nothing. And then there are these strange jumpsuits. I can't fathom any of it.

I try to be cautious. It must be that I am supposed to know this woman. Then to let on that I can't remember her will make me vulnerable. So I am non-committal, saying only "Hello" in response to her greeting.

She continues, "I'm here to help you on the trip back."

I nod. I am more confused. I am slipping into the quicksands of uncertainty.

"I'm from Leland Anderson's office," she adds.

"Oh yes, sure," I say. But it is a charade.

Nothing is sure. That last name, Anderson, has some significance, but I can't remember what. I need more time. If I could just focus on the frozen toes, and that name, Anderson, I know I would have the answer.

Suddenly there is a terrible pain. It begins with tingling in my legs, intensifies as it runs up my spine. Pain, too, has significance. I want to remember, but I can't.

I look up to see the woman studying me with pale blue eyes. "We're ready to go whenever you are, Mr. Minton," she says.

I hesitate, then respond, "Whenever you say." The words sound like they've come from miles away and grown weary on their journey.

She takes my arm and starts me toward the amfocrapht. The white surface is slippery. After two or three steps I have lost my footing and am falling. John comes up on the other side and breaks the fall. He sandwiches me between the woman and himself.

As we walk, I try to think about my age. I feel old, unsteady, unbearably, frighteningly old. I feel like some old man, in an old suit and an ancient tweed overcoat being supported by two young people. I have a vision of myself being taken to an old age home. And yet I can remember being forty, and I can't remember being any older.

The feeling of being out of place intensifies when I am inside the amfocrapht. The interior of the vehicle is just as alien as the exterior, perhaps more so. Walls, floors and ceiling are made from a material I don't recognize, reminiscent of leather, but also of plastic. All seats face away from the wall, and overhead, in front of each seat is something which looks like a window shade.

When I have been helped into one of the seats and am strapped in with a chest restraint, the woman says, "I guess you must be pretty tired, Mr. Minton."

"Yes, I am," I say. The fog seems to be rolling further down into my mind. The assault of this strangeness is more than I can bear.

"You may feel better if you rest for a while," she says. "It's not a very long ride. If you fall asleep, I'll wake you when we're there."

"Yes, yes," I say, "yes." The questions flicker in my mind, dying candles. Where are we going? Why? Who is this woman?

But I am tired, and I don't have the energy to question, and I'm not sure that I want to know the answers. And the fog is full. I fall asleep, or dream.

II

Over New Hampshire/February 15, 2008/
11:30 A.M.

When I open my eyes, the window shade is down in front of the woman's seat. The clear color image on the shade fascinates me, and I watch it over the arm of my chair for several minutes. I can see the picture but hear no sound, the sound must be set for individual reception, somewhere near the viewer's ear.

I've never seen anything quite like this before. Is it television? Is it a motion picture projection? The questions form and dissolve.

Finally the woman turns her head. She catches sight of me staring, and says, "I guess they didn't have shade screens in your day, did they,

Mr. Minton?"

In my day? What does she mean? What is she talking about? Her question doesn't make sense.

In a moment, she touches the screen. The picture disappears and the shade rolls itself up, exposing her young face to the glare of the overhead light. There seems to be an expression of concern in that face. She looks at me and asks, "Did you have a good rest? Are you feeling better now?"

"Yes, yes, thank you," I say.

"We should be arriving in Hanover in about ten minutes," she continues. "They'll give you the BHT this afternoon, keep you in the hospital overnight for observation, and tomorrow we'll go to New York."

My sight flickers. BHT, hospital, observation. What does it mean? What does any of it mean. I am in too deep; I am drowning. With all the energy I can summon, I say, "I don't understand."

"Excuse me," she says, bending toward me to hear better over the whir of the amfocrapht motor.

"I don't understand. I don't understand."

"What don't you understand? What's troubling you, Mr. Minton?"

I try to think, but my eyes fill with water and I am sobbing convulsively.

The young woman leans over me, her hand on my shoulder. "It's a strain," she says, "I know it must be a strain for you, to have been frozen for all that time, to find things so different . . . "

To have been frozen. To have been frozen, that is the key. Clarity came slowly. As I sob, I remember Cryo Genius, that place in the mountains in New York. And I remember Tomasso, and the nurse, Gertrude. The fog lifts further. I remember Smedly and the frozen north of Hudson Bay.

As sobbing relieves the tension, remembrance relieves the fear. I am able to carry my recollections back further, deeper. I remember the reason for being frozen. It was an incurable disease. I had an incurable disease and that's why I went to be frozen. The disease, Hays Syndrome, that is part of my being. "Has it been cured, then?" I ask, "Has Hays Syndrome been cured?"

"The cure was recently discovered in Hanover," she responds. "It's a massive dose of BHT, five thousand mg, I think. That's why we're going directly there. They're going to take care of the cure today. Tomorrow, as I said, we'll go to New York."

Strength begins to return. I stop sobbing. Still, I am disturbed by the acute differences between this environment and the one I remember living in. There is the amfocrapht, and the shade screens and the unisex jumpsuits with their diagonal row of snaps. Lapse of time. "What year is this?" I ask.

"2008."

A cold chill runs up my back and lodges in my neck. Is it the disease or the revelation? I can't tell. I have felt ever since emerging from that building in Hudson Bay that things were strange. Now, I have the explanation. More than thirty years have passed since I last breathed fresh air. I slept longer than Rip Van Winkle. Still, understanding is the first step in dealing with this new environment and its problems. I feel stronger.

Other questions need answers. "Excuse me," I say to the young woman, "but who are you, then?"

She laughs. It is a full warm laugh. Her blue eyes smile at me. "I'm Janet Helson, your lawyer," she says. Then she laughs again. "I'm one of the junior people in Leland Anderson's office. I was given the job of going to Hudson Bay to accompany you on your trip back into the real world. Mr. Anderson is really not that well these days. A trip like this would have been out of the question for him."

The answer explains much, but it also focuses me on other questions, other problems. I think of Leland Anderson. He must have been fifty when I saw him last. That would put him in his mid-eighties. Again I feel a tingling chill in my back.

Then, looking at this young woman, I think of Mary. She would be in her mid-sixties, now. It is incongruous. "Do you know if my wife is alive, Miss Helson?"

"Yes, she is," says Janet Helson, and nothing more. At that moment the loud drone of the amfocrapht changes pitch and the behicles begins its descent to Hanover, New Hampshire. A few minutes later I am in the Hanover Hospital receiving a massive dose of BHT.

III

Hanover/February 16, 2008/8:49 A.M.

"I thought I was only going to be here overnight," I say, sounding, even to myself, a little
like a spoiled child.

"Well, it's a little more complex than we
thought at first," says the young woman. "When
we saw you yesterday we didn't know you had
been frozen twice. That makes a big difference,
you know. One freezing produces a certain a-
mount of cell deterioration; two freezings produce considerably more. I want to make sure
that we've done as much restoration as possible
before we let you out."

"Well, how long is it going to be then,

doctor, before I get out?"

She shakes her head. She smiles and says, "Can't say for sure. If your condition continues stable we'll ask for government clearance for your release in two or three days. Meanwhile you keep eating those maraschino cherries. We'll see how things go."

"What's the point of those cherries anyway? They're a strange supplement to the regular diet here."

"Lots of preservatives. Very good for cell restoration."

I sit up in the cramped bed. I feel fine. The tingling is gone. There is no more pain. Even the numbness where three toes had been is disappearing. But I want to be sure. "The Hays Syndrome," I say, "what about that?"

The doctor smiles again. "Oh, that," she says, "You can forget about that. No question about it, BHT does the trick. We've done a number of administrations. No problem. You're cured of that."

I'm doubtful. This killer disease, it can't be dismissed so lightly, I'm sure. "But how do you know?" I say. "Don't you even do a residual mylotar test?" The words tumble out. I'm not even sure I know what residual mylotar is or where I have heard the term before, but the term is right. I know that.

The doctor laughs again, this time in a way that seems self-conscious. "No, Mr. Minton, we don't do a residual mylotar test," she says. "That was a torture chamber devised by a couple of

English faddists. It was given up years ago. I can assure you it isn't the least bit necessary."

The young physician puts her arthoscope in a pocket over her firm breast and she starts to leave. "Another question," I call. "I find my mind is very foggy. Sometimes I can't remember things right. Can anything be done about that?"

"That's one of the things we're working on," she says. "It's a symptom of the cell deterioration. You keep up the cherries. Can you stomach preserved ginger?" She doesn't wait for a response, but adds, "I'll prescribe some of that. You try it; it's very good for this sort of problem."

Again she starts to leave. Again I call her back. "Listen, doc," I say. "If I'm going to have to stay here for a few days, don't you think you can do something about this bed? It's impossible."

"Too soft?" she asks, pressing her hand on the mattress, near the foot of the bed.

"No, too short," I grumble. "Are you people all midgets? How are you supposed to sleep on a four-foot long bed?"

"Fetal position, Mr. Minton, fetal position. All the tests have shown that it's the best for the body," she says. "You might find you like it."

"I'm too old to change. I slept on a regular bed for forty years, and I was frozen in a straight out position for another thirty-three, and that counts for something, too. Please, if you can find an old fashioned bed I'd really appreciate it."

"I'll report the problem to the adminis-
121

trative office. They'll do what they can," says
the doctor. She leaves.

IV

Hanover/February 16, 2008/11:35 A.M.

"Lunch."

I have been dozing, fitfully. The aide's one word announcement of meal service wakes me. The tray sits on the service rest in front of me. It mocks me. It challenges me to come and be a part of the twenty-first century.

There are three small plastic cups on the tray. In one are the yellow flakes which seem to form the staple of the diet. They look like soap flakes and dissolve in the mouth into glue. I have been told that they are egg substitute flakes and provide full protein allowances for healthy people.

Another cup has a small quantity of a light blue gruel. The aide yesterday explained that it is called mock vegetable melange and is a fortified supplement providing the full spectrum of vitamins and minerals. It tastes like blue gruel, with a suggestion of copper.

The third cup has two large brown tablets, the coffee gel tablets, which one is supposed to eat instead of coffee.

The tray has two other delights, incongruities sitting next to the blue gruel and the egg substitute flakes. There is the full bottle of maraschino cherries. I have been admonished to eat as many of these as I can. And there is a small jar of preserved ginger.

Some lunch.

I try eating, mixing the modern with the old, cherries with gruel. I find myself looking around the room, cataloguing the different. The room is small, much smaller than hospital rooms I remember. The four-foot bed takes up most of the floor area. I wonder whether they'd even be able to fit a traditional bed in the room.

I study the wall console, with its tubes, buttons and toggle switches. It reminds me of the console I used to dread facing in the dentist's chair. And up near the ceiling on the far wall is a shade screen, rolled up like the ones on the amfocrapht.

The more closely I study these things, the more disturbed I become. The new technologies, the new foods, they all remind me of my dislocation, of the fact that I am now living in a time and place which I don't really understand.

The view outside gives consolation, though. It is the past, familiar. Snow is falling from a gray New Hampshire sky. As it falls it covers the ground and obscures the paths.

I have finished my lunch and pushed the tray away. I am watching the sky, the snow, when there is a knock on the door. It is Janet Helson, bright and cheerful as yesterday.

"How are you today, Mr. Minton?" she says, brushing the snow off the arms and shoulders of her yellow jumpsuit.

"Much better," I say, "much better." Her arrival has broken the spell of the falling snow. "It looks like I have a clean bill of health on the Hays Syndrome. Completely cured, the doctor said this morning. But I have to stay here a few days longer, something about having been frozen twice, I think."

"Yes," she said, nodding. "I'm afraid you're kind of a medical oddity. Plenty of people have been frozen and thawed, but I don't think there are very many who have done it twice. The doctors probably want to check you over as carefully as possible, to see the effects of a second freezing."

I find myself laughing, my spirits lifted. There is something about this girl which strikes a chord, something direct and open. She is my first window on this new world. I haven't yet decided how I feel about 2008, but I have already decided that there is something refreshing about Janet Helson.

125

"Well," I say, "I think one day is long enough in the hospital. I've had enough of this room, and this bed, particularly this bed. I can't take a four-foot bed."

"I'm afraid you'll have to get used to it," she says. "They don't make long beds anymore. I doubt that you could find any around, except maybe in a Retrieved Association Museum. Now you wouldn't like to end up living in a museum, would you, Mr. Minton?"

"No. I guess not," I say. I am grinning; the force of her logic has delighted me. Then I reflect and add, "I don't know. I'm not so sure. If things are really so different, maybe I'll be happier in a museum."

"Try the real world first," she responds.

"What about the food. Don't you eat anything else besides soap flakes and blue gruel?"

"Oh, we have a pretty varied diet," says Miss Helson, defensively. "True most of it is made up of pastes and flakes and dispensable gels, but it fills our nutritional needs completely. None of the hit and miss nutrition of the 20th century. No more reliance on natural foods, the quality is so uneven."

I am learning about the predicates of the year 2008.

Miss Helson folds down the stool from the carpeted wall and perches herself on it. "Now, if you don't mind, Mr. Minton, a little business," she says.

She takes a small pad and a pen from her miniature attache case. "We've been having a little bit of trouble with your government clearance," she says. "Apparently there was no authorization certificate for your freezing in the first place. That raises a problem, you know. I wondered if you might have some ideas about the authorization certificate, how it might have been that none was issued."

I find the questions make me impatient. "Well, your office would have all the records," I say. "Leland Anderson took care of everything. In our day this wasn't something that was government controlled; in fact the government didn't know anything about it, so I don't know how there could have been an authorization certificate issued by the government. I certainly don't remember any talk about one."

"I intend to discuss the matter with Mr. Anderson," explains Miss Helson, "but he only comes into the office once or twice a week. We'll see what we can do. Maybe we can get some mileage from the fact that you were frozen in Canada. I don't know."

"What happens if the authorization can't be found, if there was no authorization? What then?" The problem intrigues me in a morbid way.

"There would be problems," she says. She is serious, glum. "There would be problems, but let's not worry about that just yet. Meanwhile, I think you've had enough of a visit from me. I have some work to do, and I'll be back with some more business later. Right now, you rest for a while. Ring for a soprific, if you like."

With that, she gets up off the stool and it folds back into the wall. She leaves. And I am alone, with another worry, an authorization certificate.

V

Hanover/February 16, 2008/4:20 P.M.

As promised, Miss Helson returns, carrying the small attache case.

"Any word on the authorization certificate, yet?" I ask.

"No, nothing," she says. "I'll tell you what, I'll make a deal with you. I'll worry about that, and you can devote all your time to worrying about four-foot long beds and blue gruel. Okay?"

I laugh. "Okay."

Again she perches herself on the stool. This time she pulls a small strip of film from her case. She presses a button in the wall console and feeds the film into a narrow aperture in the wall.

While I watch, the shade screen descends silently across the room from the bed. There is projected on it the clearly readable page of a printed document. It begins with the words, *The affidavit of 105-40-0872, also known as Dennis Minton.*

"I am projecting your affidavit on the shade screen here," she explains. "The original is on micro-mini-fiche, of course. Can you read it, or would you like me to read it for you, Mr. Minton?"

"Thanks very much," I say, "but I still do remember how to read." I am annoyed at what I take to be an implied suggestion that literacy was not a requirement for life in the middle of the twentieth century.

"I'm sorry, Mr. Minton," she says. "I didn't mean to sound patronizing. I just thought that since you had never used a shade screen before, this might seem a little strange to you."

"It is strange," I say, "strange and new fangled, but I would like to try reading it myself, to see if I can do it." I smile at her and add, "By the way, is it old fashioned to call people by their first names, Janet?"

She smiles. "Not at all, Dennis. Not at all."

Slowly I begin reading aloud from the projection on the shade screen. As I finish a page, Janet pushes a button and the next page is projected. So it goes, page by page, until the entire text has been flashed on the screen.

The affidavit is pretty dry reading, typically legal documentation. It recites the history of the

Dennis Minton Trust shortly before the original freezing at Cryo Genius. It explains that the trust instrument requires that all remaining principal of the trust be paid to me upon my being thawed and cured of Hays Syndrome. It contains a certification by me that I have indeed been thawed and cured of the disease and am thereby claiming the trust property as my own.

When I finish reading it, I say, "Sounds all right. But how do I go about signing a picture on a shade screen?"

Janet laughs. "Signing," she says, "is a lot simpler than it seems. All you need is a micromini-stylus, and I just happen to have one." From the attache case she pulls a small black box. A pen sticks out of one side of the box. Into the other side she puts the film which she has retrieved from the wall unit. Then she places the entire thing in front of me and says, "Sign your number first, then your name."

I don't understand. "Excuse me," I say, "What do you mean?"

"I said sign your number first, and then your name," she says casually. I look at her. I still want to question, but she adds, "Your number, your registration number, you know."

"Do you mean that number up at the start of the affidavit?" I ask, a little uncertainly.

"Yes, of course," Janet says.

"We used to call that a Social Security number," I say, almost wistfully. "What do you need that for?"

"Yes," says Janet. "It used to be called a

131

Social Security number, and then for a while they called it a Taxpayer Identification number, I believe. Now it's an IRN, an Individual Registration Number, but it's all the same thing. Nowadays, the government makes you put it on almost everything. It's a means of identifying everyone, keeping track of everyone. It's pretty important."

I take hold of the pen. I am about to start writing. But I hesitate, saying, "You know, I can't remember my number."

"You'll remember it soon enough," says Janet. "You have to use it often enough." She opens her file, finds the number and reads it off to me. I try to commit it to memory.

When I have finished, I ask, "Now what happens with this piece of film?"

"I prepared it this afternoon, and had you sign it today," explains Janet, "so that I could send it down to New York and get the legal proceedings started as soon as possible. This little piece of film is the first stage in the lawsuit. This way we'll be able to go forward even though you are still in the hospital for a few more days."

"And what do the legal proceedings consist of? What is this lawsuit all about?"

"Quite simple," explains Janet. "Shortly before you were frozen the first time at Cryo Genius, the day before, I think, you put most of your assets, about four million dollars, into a trust fund. Leland Anderson and the bank were the Trustees. They were directed, by the terms of the trust, to pay the expenses of freezing you, the costs of keeping you frozen, thawing you and

132

curing you of Hays Syndrome. While you were frozen, whatever income wasn't needed to pay the cost of keeping you frozen was to be paid to your wife, Mary."

I nod to show that I am following the explanation.

Janet continues, "The trust provides that as soon as you are thawed and cured of the disease, the entire trust is to be paid directly to you. The law requires that the Trustees get the court's approval before they can make the final payment to you. The purpose of the affidavit is to request that approval."

I have listened carefully and understood the explanation completely. I have also had time to admire Janet's blue eyes, her long brown hair, and the fit of the one piece jumpsuit which covers but doesn't conceal, a young well formed body.

Finally I say, "I have two questions. Question One: How much is this trust worth now?"

"About nine and a half million dollars," says Janet casually.

"In the middle of the twentieth century that would have been a lot of money. Is it still a lot?"

"Oh, yes," responds Janet. "Quite a lot. With the deflation we've had over the last few years, I'm sure that nine and a half million will go a good deal further today than it would have in your day." She pauses, then gives me a smile and adds, "Dennis, you're very comfortable, fixed for life. You really don't have to worry. You won't have to work, unless of course you want to."

"Question Two, where is my wife?"

"That's a harder question to deal with," she says. The smile has left her face. She pauses. She looks like a diver gulping air before jumping into the sea. "Mary is living in an Elderly People's Residence," she says. "You have to remember, Dennis, she is 65." Another gulp of air, another dive. "There's something else about Mary that you ought to know. After you were frozen up at Hudson Bay, Mary brought legal proceedings, and she had you declared legally dead. Then she married the County Attorney who had handled the Cryo Genius case, Peter Dwyer."

"I see." I am relieved, but at the same time uneasy. I have a sense of fear, something I don't quite fathom has gone amiss.

VI

Hanover/February 21, 2008/8:35 A.M.

"I can give you a prescription for the cherries and also for the ginger," says the doctor.
"You should keep up with both of them. They've
been very helpful in your case."

"Thanks, doctor," I respond. "Are there any
other of the old fashioned foods you might be
able to prescribe for me?"

She laughs. "Oh, you'll get used to egg substitute flakes. Anyway, they're much better for
you. If you want food the way it used to be, try
the Retrieved Association museum."

She has just completed my final physical
and, in effect, discharged me, as completely

recovered, both from Hays Syndrome and the effects of two freezings.

"Oh, one last thing," she says. "About those toes. Now anytime you want a plasticene job done, for cosmetic purposes, just call the plasticene department of a local hospital, and make an appointment. It's really an out patient procedure, local anesthetic, quite simple."

"Do you think it's necessary?" I ask.

"No, not necessary," she says. "Purely cosmetic, it'll give you the look of the three missing toes, that's all. But you might want to have it done."

"Thanks for the advice; thanks for everything, in fact," I say.

"Oh, you're welcome. It's just my job," she says. With a wave she is gone.

I am free to dress. It proves more difficult than I expected. At my request, Janet brought me new clothes, modern clothes. First I put on the net-like one piece undergarment. It reminds me of ski underwear. The material is made from some chemical base and is extremely lightweight. Once I have put it on it is quite comfortable.

Then there is the blue jumpsuit. It is bulky, difficult to get on, but once on it too is quite comfortable. Finally I put on the strange blue plastic shoes. They snap on to the jumpsuit. I walk around the room and find the heelless shoes uncomfortable. They will take a little bit of getting used to.

When Janet arrives I feel I am halfway to being a man of 2008. "Well, you look just fine in your new clothes," she says, "how do they feel?"

"Strange, uncomfortable, alien," I respond, "but I'm going to keep at it. I'll get used to them."

"Sure you will," she says with encouragement. "The jumpsuits are really great. There's nothing else you ever have to wear. It puts clothing in the proper perspective." Then she adds, "Are you ready to go?"

"I've been ready for five days," I say, "and I do have doctor's permission."

"Good," says Janet. "I have some good news, start your life on the outside world right. We solved the problem about the authorization certificate. There is a government bureau called the Non-certificate Freezings Bureau. Most of the cases they deal with are criminal situations, people who failed to get authorization because they were fugitives. Well, we were able to get an authorization waiver from them, on the grounds that the Hudson Bay facility had not been required to obtain authorizations in 1978 for freezings. It was a little tricky, but one of the partners at the firm knows a couple of the fellows at the Bureau."

"Does that mean I'm legal?" I ask.

"It means that your freezing and thawing has now been certified as just as legal as if it had been undertaken with proper authorization. And I think it's time we catch the amfocrapht for New York."

And we are off. Out of an environment which has become secure and known over the last few days. Once more into the unknown, the uncertain.

VII

New York/February 22, 2008/10:31 A.M.

Janet warned me more than once that Anderson is an old man. But I never really understood the fact. I heard Janet tell me that Anderson was more than eighty, but it was an abstrac-
tion, it meant nothing, until I finally find myself
standing in front of Anderson's desk.

It is the same desk I remember from the old
Park Avenue offices. The rosewood and steel once
looked so sleek and modern. Now it is a relic, faded and incongruous in a room with carpeted walls
and the ubiquitous shade screen.

Behind the desk is the strangest incongruity
of all: Anderson. Or is it Anderson? It looks to

me like Anderson in the stage make-up of an old man, furrows crossing his forehead, deep lines running down his face. His eyes are more deeply set than I remember them, and his salt-and-pepper hair has been bleached a snowy white. And he is in the garb of the 21st century, the blue jumpsuit.

The experience is overwhelming. Anderson speaks a greeting. And the handshake he offers is feeble, fragile. I find I am barely able to respond. Words echo back and forth, but for a moment all I can hear is a voice in my mind saying, "Why, he is an old man. He's nothing like the man I knew."

"You look none the worse for your experience of being frozen," he says slowly. "You look no different than you did thirty-three years ago."

I wish I could return the compliment. But to do so would mock him. Thirty-three years have ravaged his face. I say only, "It's been a long time."

Anderson adjusts himself in the large chair. He seems to have shriveled over the years. "Now we have to get this trust thing cleared up for you," he says, "and then you're pretty well free to pick up where you left off."

"Not quite," I say, looking into the pools of his eyes. "Everyone's that much older. I suppose many of the people I knew are dead. I hear that Mary is married to someone else."

"Yes," says Anderson. It is almost a whisper. "Thirty-three years is a long time." He wheezes slightly, then he nods to Janet and adds, "Miss Helson is taking good care of you, I hope. Sorry I can't do it myself, but I don't get to the office as often now as I'd like to."

"Oh, Janet is doing fine, just fine," I say, exchanging smiles with her. "She's helped me over a lot of the rough spots, explaining a lot of things to me. There have been quite a few changes over the last thirty-three years, some of them a little difficult to get used to. We came down from Hanover by amfocrapht yesterday. It's the second amfocrapht ride I've had, but I'll need a few more before I'm used to them."

"I've been using them for years, and I'm still not used to them," says the old man. "And where are you staying now?"

"I have a room at Hotel Complex No. 3, but Janet suggests that I apply for permanent housing as quickly as possible."

"Good, good," says Anderson, his voice drifting away. He coughs. "You will have to come and have dinner at my place one evening." Again the voice trails off.

I thank him. It is clear that the old man is already growing weary. The interview has perhaps been too much for him. I soon terminate it.

As I leave Anderson's office I understand fully for the first time that Anderson is old. We had been contemporaries; our pasts were intertwined, but now a generation or more separates us.

I find it depressing, this dislocation from my own past, this loss of identification and identity.

"Anderson's so old," I say to Janet. "I wasn't really prepared for that."

"Go on over to the Retrieved Association

Museum," says Janet. "That might cheer you up. I'll meet you there, on the 1970s floor, in about an hour."

Good suggestion.

VIII

New York/February 22, 2008/11:20 A.M.

I take Janet's advice. I follow her detailed directions and soon I am on the people mover, a moving belt with seats which serves the mass transportation function.

I feel conspicuous with the crowds. I am uncomfortable in the blue jumpsuit. I feel I am not wearing it properly. It seems to pinch and pull in the wrong places.

I think that people are staring at me, at my short hair, still close cropped from the pre-freezing procedures. But as I sit on the people mover, I calm myself. My suit is a perfect match to those worn by all the other men, except the government personnel who wear green. Looking closely, I realize that the blank faces are not watching me, they are merely focusing absently on the side of the tunnel.

Following Janet's instructions, I watch the off points. The museum's off point is well marked. I walk from the mover to the adjoining moving platform of the off point. That takes me to the exit, which just happens to be the lobby of the Museum of the Retrieved Association of the City of New York.

I study the directory long enough to discover that the eighth floor is devoted to the 1970s. I take the elevator. When the silent doors open, I suddenly find myself in a different time.

I am struck first by the smell. It is familiar, remembered. I can't quite identify all the elements that make it up, but I can close my eyes and remember places. It might be Leland Anderson's office of 1978, or my own office, or a hundred other offices I've been in. It is a subtle distillate of stale cigarette smoke, sweating typewriters and an overworked air conditioning system.

And the visual stimulation is a perfect match to the smell. The area simulates the reception room of a 1970s office: four cumbersome chairs placed at discrete intervals on an old Oriental rug. There is abstract art on the walls, air conditioning vents in the ceiling humming audibly, and a well-scrubbed young lady at the reception desk with a telephone key switchboard.

The young lady has long blonde hair and wears an attractive skirt and blouse. No jumpsuits here, just traditional 1970s attire. I feel out of place in my regulation blues.

"Can I help you?" she says with a warm smile.

The question perplexes me. I thought I came to the museum to study artifacts, relics of the past, but I find myself with a sense of *deja vu*. Is this a museum or a trip back in time? Finally I say, "I want to see the 1970s exhibit."

"Please have a seat, won't you?" says the young lady, almost without acknowledging my response. "Mr. Poore will be with you in a moment."

My confusion is compounded. I didn't ask to see Mr. Poore, yet I have been told to wait for him. Dutifully, I do so. I sit in the deep suede chair. Carelessly, my eyes catch a pile of magazines on the end table. They are almost new. They look familiar. I pick one up. It is *Time*, and bears the date, September 16, 1970. The date startles me. This is indeed a trip back. It is as if, in this enclosed space, time has been turned back on itself, and I am sitting again in a familiar office waiting room of the early 1970s.

In a moment a short young man wearing a wide-lapeled jacket and a broad-striped tie is approaching me with a hand outstretched. "Hi!" he says, "I'm Ken Poore. Welcome to the 1970s!"

Poore speaks quickly. He bounces out at me from some side door and bounds back again, beckoning me to follow. There is a small cubicle of an office. Very 1970s. Traditional desk and telephone, all the other items I remember from

145

twentieth century offices. No shade screens, no carpeted walls, none of the intrusions of the year 2008.

"What can I do for you?" says Poore, seated behind his Danish modern desk.

"I was curious to see the exhibit of the 1970s," I respond. I am feeling uncomfortable. This office and the reception area are faithful re-creations of the past, but that is it. They are nothing more than re-creations.

"Well, this is it," says Poore. "Yes sir, this is it. Aren't you familiar with the organic museum concept?"

"Organic museum?" I ask. I am even more confused.

"Yes," says Poore. "This is an organic museum. No exhibits behind glass cases. The experience is the museum. Here we have recreated the life of the 1970s. Our re-creation is a living organic museum. We are constantly updating, refining what we do. Quite a number of researchers are working on the period. And then, of course, we have the oral histories prepared by the Retrieved."

"I see," I respond, but I remain confused. I hesitate, shifting my eyes from the onyx desk set to the floor and back again to the desk set. Finally, I say, "By the way, you wouldn't know where I could get a 1970s type bed, would you?"

Poore leans back in his chair and laughs. "You're one of the Retrieved, then?" he asks.

"I guess so," I say. But I am embarrassed. My eyes avert his gaze.

146

"It's nothing to be ashamed of," says Poore, opening a desk drawer and pulling out some long printed forms. "I'm a Retrieved myself, you know." He lowers his voice to a more confidential level, leans across the desk and says, "We're a pretty special bunch, you know. There aren't too many from the seventies. Then he adds, "Have you registered yet?"

"No. Am I supposed to?"

"Oh, yes, you must. Every Retrieved has to register with the Association. I've got a set of the forms right here. You just fill them out and turn them in, as soon as possible." He passes half a dozen papers across the desk. I am relieved to see that they don't use micro-mini-fiche films for this purpose.

Then Poore tells me about his own freezing in 1978. He was a reporter for one of the national news magazines. An assignment backfired mysteriously, and he ended up frozen for 27 years. Retrieved in 2005 he came to work for the Association almost immediately.

Poore points out that freezing was only in its infancy in the 1970s. As a result, there are only a few thousand Retrieved from that period. Most of the two million Retrieved are from the 1980s and 1990s when the Formal Freeze Banks were established.

Poore takes me under his wing, giving me a personal tour of the balance of the 1970s Museum. There is the 1973 living room. It has a working imitation wood burning fireplace, which burns simulations. There is also a vintage television set. Visitors can relax on the couch or in the chairs and enjoy tapes of 1970s television fare, carefully selected by the researchers for the authenticity and broad spectrum appeal.

There is a boutique with artifacts and gifts, and a small art gallery for collectors. The motion picture theatre specializes in films from the 1970s but also, I am told, offers a good dose of earlier movie fare, including some silent pictures.

The finest re-creation of the museum, Poore's special pride, it seems, is the final stop of the tour. It is the snack shop, a special fast food emporium which, he tells me, re-creates the vibrant textures and flavors of the fast food franchises of the seventies. Poore explains that all of the foods are made from extruded soypaste, one of the basics of twenty-first century diet, but coloring and moulding has been so deftly effected that the eye is deceived. The taste, too, is a painstaking re-creation of the tastes of the seventies, the cardboard and paste hamburger and the chalklike milk shake.

At Poore's insistence, I taste the hamburger, but I can't really appreciate the thoroughness of the re-creation. While I lived in New York in the 1970s, I ate almost exclusively at the old French or continental restaurants in the city. I was never inside a fast food chain store before this museum visit. So I have no standard by which to compare the hamburger.

While we are drinking our vanilla milk shakes Poore explains the advantage of a strong Retrieved Association. "The Association provides us

148

with a lot of things we miss from the old days," he says.

Just then, Janet arrives, as she promised.

"Dennis," she says, "I thought I'd find you at the food. Trying to get a little change from egg substitute flakes, are you?"

I laugh and introduce her to Poore. Greetings are exchanged, but there is something strange about Janet. It is as if she is uncomfortable with the trappings of the twentieth century, as if she feels she is in an alien environment. She seems disturbed by the plastic tables and chairs and the plastic food of the hamburger stand.

Poore offers to get her a milk shake and some traditional soggy french fries. He leaves. I turn to Janet and ask, "Is something the matter? Do you feel uncomfortable here?"

"No," she says. "It's not that." She pauses and looks away. Then she catches my eye and says, "I'm afraid I have some news, some bad news. Mary, your wife, your former wife, I guess, is dead."

What's bad about that, I find myself thinking. Mary had seemed a supreme inconvenience. To have her out of the way is a simple solution to the problems her existence raised. But I suppress this reaction. Janet looks at me so soberly; her look chides me. I am contrite and ask, "When's the funeral?"

At the mention of a funeral Janet's face seems to relax. "I'm afraid we don't believe in those rituals any more," she says.

"No funerals?" I ask in disbelief.

"No," she says. "It's a custom that I've read about in the history books; I know they used to do it, but not any more. I don't think there have been any funerals since the Undertaker Scandals of the 1990s. A lot of seamy practices were uncovered, and funerals just stopped being the custom. It may even be that they became illegal. Then there was the growth of the Transplant Banks and the Freeze Banks, those may have had something to do with it too. Now, when a person dies, the Recycling Service collects the body and disposes of it."

"I see." I am finishing the last of my milk shake and considering the strangeness of this new world. After a pause, I add, "But how did you find out about Mary?"

Janet leans closer to me, with animation she explains the new customs to a stranger. "Our office subscribes to a weekly death list service," she explains. "We check it over pretty carefully. It's good business. This week's list had Mary's name on it. By the way, she died last week, the same day that you were thawed. There is a certain irony to that, isn't there?"

Before I can respond, Poore has returned with Janet's milk shake and french fries. The conversation returns to the Retrieved Association and the things it can do for me. Lots of things.

My mind wanders while the two others talk. Experiencing the studied 1970s feeling of the Museum snack shop I realize that Mary's death is merely a symbol, a reminder that the past is gone completely. It can be re-created in a museum, but it can't be revived.

IX

I have accepted the invitation out of curiosity more than anything else, but now I regret it. Anderson is a boring old man. He drones on about the past, some of it a past we shared and some of it quite foreign to me. But even talk of the deals we made, and the money we made, bores me.

I am curious to see how he lives. Hopeful, I suppose, that I will find a private Retrieved Association Museum. But it is no such thing. True, he doesn't wear the jumpsuit which I saw him in at the office. Instead there is an old sport coat over a turtle neck. The coat looks threadbare,

151

something he must have bought years ago before they stopped making them.

Dinner is served in a wood-panelled room. Brass sconces are lit with beeswax candles. The candle light gives a glow to the silver. At one end of the oval table sits Anderson, at the other me. We are alone, except for the cook, who serves.

With seeming pride she brings us each steaming bowls of a clear liquid. It is packaged plasma gel, an all purpose nutrient. I remember it from the hospital dietician's lectures.

While I sip the plasma gel, Anderson talks about Mary. "Oh yes," he says, in a weak voice, "I was very sorry to hear about Mary. Terrible thing: she's not that old either, only 64 or 65 I think."

He slurps at the soup, and continues. "She was a strange person, always was, if you don't mind my saying so. Why, I remember the first time you were frozen and I told her, her only concern was the money, what would happen to your money. She was pretty relieved when I explained there was a trust and she was well protected. But that was the only thing she could think about, the money. No concern about the danger to you." He slurps on and the voice gurgles into the soup.

Since he raised the subject, I pursue it. "What was the story about Mary's remarriage? I heard she married again."

"Oh, yes, that was another thing," says Anderson. "After you were frozen the second time, up in Canada, she told me she wanted to do some-

152

hing, she wanted me to assert her rights. I told her that I was your lawyer, and as far as I could see, she had no rights which could be asserted against you, but I suggested she see another lawyer." He slurps some more soup, and then, "She evidently went to this Dwyer fellow, Peter Dwyer. He had been the prosecutor for the Tomasso case up in White Ridge. They became fast friends.

Anderson has warmed to the story. He speaks rapidly, sometimes too rapidly and he coughs on his own words.

"Dwyer thought up the idea of having you declared legally dead. Very clever from her point of view. It gave her the freedom to remarry and it gave her a crack at your estate. She wanted to get your will offered for probate until I explained that everything was in the trust and the trust could not be touched until you were thawed."

"So you think she was just money hungry?" I ask across the table. An old suspicion is being confirmed.

"No question about it," says Anderson. For emphasis he slaps his spoon into the bowl. "But she got hers. Dwyer got wind of the trust, and the fact that if something happened to her, she could designate who would take the trust after she was gone, and he pursued her and married her and as far as I've heard, he angled for years to get her to name him her beneficiary."

The soup is removed. In its place the cook offers extruded soypaste squares and blue gruel. My heart sinks. Blue gruel on expensive English

153

china. It's too much.

I try to take my mind off the food, returning to the conversation. "But Mary's designation is valueless, now that I've been thawed and cured. Isn't that so?"

"Precisely," says Anderson. "Dwyer will get nothing for his troubles, except old age." He laughs and scoops up some gruel with his spoon. I wonder whether one is supposed to comment on the food, even though it is obvious that it has come from the dispensers.

Finally, I say, "Do you ever have a longing for some of the old foods, steak and baked potatoes, good boiled Maine lobster, something like that?"

"Not really. No," says Anderson. "I quite enjoy blue gruel, always have."

The subject is closed, and I am afraid I have insulted his cuisine.

Dinner concludes with coffee gel tablets and pudding flakes. The flakes are pink and green and distinctly soapy. I have never had these particular flakes before and make a mental note never to have them again.

Anderson drones on about the past, his past.

After dinner we sit in old chairs in the library and sip bottled water from small snifters. The purity of the moment escapes me. I am pleased when the old man soon slips into gentle slumber. I am able to tiptoe out, leaving my apologies and thanks with the cook. I shall remember not to dine again at Leland Anderson's.

X

New York/February 27, 2008/10:40 A.M.

"I don't understand this. I don't understand this at all," I protest as I am directed into the small room with the gray quilted walls. "What's the meaning of this?"

"Just routine, routine questions," says the other. "Just have to ask you a few routine questions, if you know what I mean. Them's the rules." There is something about him, about the grossness of his figure, bulging the seams of the green government jumpsuit, that reminds me of someone. The tilt of the face, the gestures strike a chord in my memory. But I haven't quite placed him.

"What do you mean, 'routine questions'?" I respond. "I haven't done anything wrong. You have no right to take me from my room at the hotel like that and bring me here on mere suspicion."

"Them's the rules," repeats the other. "The state has an interest in every life and every death, if you know what I mean. One Mary Minton Dwyer died recently. You used to be married to her. We thought you might have an interest in seeing her dead. You gotta be questioned. Sit down."

I sit in the hard straight chair in the center of the room. The other flips a switch near the door. The room is cast in darkness. There is another click and a piercing white quartz light plays on my face. It pulses in intensity as the other speaks.

"State your number and name, for the record," he says.

"Must I do this," I respond. "Don't I have a right to call my lawyer, to remain silent."

"The citizen has no rights. Don't you know that, mister. Again, state your number and name."

"I can't remember my number," I say. "I keep a record of it here in my wallet. May I check that?"

"Go ahead, but make it quick," is the response.

I fumble through my wallet, find the card with the number, but have difficulty reading it without light. I bring it up to my face where the light shines brightly and read the number off to the questioner.

"Did you know the deceased, number 253-77-9804, also known as Mary Minton Dwyer?"

The light flashes and pulsates. It penetrates my brain, warming it deeply. "Yes," I say.

"Were you related to her?"

I feel myself alone, questioned by a disembodied voice and violated by a jack hammer drilling my mind. "Yes," I respond.

"How were you related to her?"

The light gnaws like teeth at the crevices of my brain. "Once she was my wife."

"When did you last see her alive?"

I find myself screaming, to be heard over the noise of the light, "More than thirty years ago. I haven't seen her in thirty years." The flashes of light seem to bounce off the back of my head. They echo within my mind. The tension presses a vice against my head.

"You killed her," says the voice. "You eliminated her so that you would have no trouble about your trust, so that all the money would be yours. Admit your guilt. Ask for mercy from the state."

I shake my head violently. I feel like I am spinning. "No, no!" I am screaming. "I haven't seen her for thirty years. I don't even know where she lived. I don't know what you're talking about." The light keeps flashing across my brain. I close my eyes. The light still flashes.

"Admit it. You killed her," says the other. "You killed her. You are an enemy of the state."

The words beat against my brain. The ligh
and sound echo. I gasp with a searing convulsion
There is a snapping in my mind, and I scream
"No! No! Tomasso! Tomasso! It's you! You'r
the enemy." I keel over.

When I awaken, I am lying on a couch. A
cross the room is a garish painting of Venice. Th
colors stir my memory. It is the same artist, I rea
ize, who did that horrible painting at Cryo Geniu
so many years ago.

Looking around, I see the burly interrogato
The green jumpsuit stretched tight across his bell
as he sits in the chair on the far side of the room
near the window.

"So it is you, Tomasso, isn't it?" I say

Tomasso fondles a fat cigar. It's the first bi
of tobacco I've seen in the year 2008. "You'v
got a good memory, there, you know," he say
"A damn good memory."

I appreciate the compliment. I am very de
fensive about my memory, afraid that the secon
freezing produced permanent damage. I eat m
maraschino cherries and my preserved ginger da
ly, and am glad of proofs that my memory reall
is working.

Looking around the room, I am perplexed.
remember the gray interrogation cubicle with th
quilted panels, and then my mind blurred. Now,
seem to be in the lounging room of someone
apartment.

"What's going on here?" I say. "How did
get here?"

"Well," responds Tomasso, "when yo

identified me, I kinda thought it might be a good idea if we came back to my place for a little chat." He walks over to the low cabinet, unlocks the door, and asks, "Would you like some water?"

"Yes, thank you," I say. I look around the room for an explanation. "I still don't know what is going on."

Tomasso fills two thimble full glasses with the sparkling clear liquid from the small bottle. He offers me a glass. "Well, you see, it's like this," he says, "I might as well tell you the whole story. I'm just an Interrogation Agent. Had this job for the last couple of years. I was frozen up in Canada the same time you were, and I was frozen for quite some time, only defrosted about five years ago, when things finally quieted down. I got some friends in the right places, so I got this job here." He sips from the small glass.

"But what's the point of interrogating me? I haven't seen Mary in over thirty years," I say.

"Well, like I told you," explains Tomasso, "them's the rules. You look at your Green Book." He pulls the small green pamphlet from his hip pocket, thmbs through it and stops at a page to read, " 'Rule 463: Any death which does not occur in a Death Care Facility must be thoroughly investigated. A full written report must be filed by the Interrogation Agent in charge of the case.' "

I get up from the couch, walk over to the window. I hope that while admiring the view, I can also determine our location. "You still have not answered, what was the point of bringing me here?"

"To be honest," says Tomasso, looking sober, "I didn't like the idea that you identified me. I thought you and I might talk about it. You see, I've got my friends in the right places, but there are some things they don't know about, and I don't think I'd like it if they found out about them."

"So you want to buy my silence?" I respond. As I speak, my eyes carefully search for landmarks I might recognize out the window. I am uncertain. It is evident that Tomasso doesn't want me to talk, but I don't know how he intends to effect this purpose.

"That's the general idea," says Tomasso. "You see, if I wanted to file a negative report in this here investigation, that would be it, curtains for you. But I'm not that sort of a guy."

"What do you mean, a negative report. You don't have anything on me. I didn't know where the woman lived. Anyway, I have a full alibi. I was in Hanover, being thawed, when she died."

"Not so fast, not so fast." Tomasso leans back into his chair. "Dennis, you never heard of agents? You never heard of telling someone else to knock someone off for you? What if I can produce a hired gun who says he killed Mary on your instructions, from Canada? What if I can produce the cash you paid him?"

"Manufactured evidence," I respond.

"Precisely," says Tomasso, "precisely, manufactured, but perfectly adequate in a court of law. You wouldn't have a defense. You wouldn't want me to do that, now would you?"

"What do you want in return?" I ask.

"I want you to keep quiet about me, but you see, Dennis, I'm kinda insecure, so I need more than your promise, I need your guarantee." He smiles as he speaks. He pours himself another thimbleful from the small bottle. Then he takes a sliver of film from the counter. "So there ain't no confusion about things," he says, "I'd like you to sign this micro-mini-fiche."

"What is it?" I ask, crossing to him.

"A confession," says Tomasso, "a confession admitting that you hired an assassin to kill Mary."

"But I didn't. You know I didn't."

"No matter," explains Tomasso. "It's just my little life insurance policy, in case your tongue starts wagging. It's my guarantee that you'll be quiet. As long as you say nothing, it's just between you and me."

I scan the confession on the shade screen. It is a pack of lies. But when the viewing is over, Tomasso brings me the stylus and I sign. Only then can I leave Tomasso's apartment.

On my way up the elevator to the amfocrapht platform, I think about the confession and Tomasso's insistence on my signing it. Where will it lead? I don't know.

XI

New York/March 1, 2008/10:23 A.M.

I am in Janet's office. For a change I delight in the new. My eyes feast on the different, on the shade screen, the side board desk and the computer terminal. It is exciting, vibrant. And in the center is Janet, the nerve source for this pulsating entity. I am enthralled by it and her.

"I'm afraid I have another affidavit for you," she says. There is a mock seriousness to her tone. She doesn't want to burden me with this nuisance.

"Another affidavit? What was wrong with the last one?" I have found the best way to keep your lawyer on the defensive is to question him.

It also keeps fees down.

"Well, Mary's death has changed things," she says.

"I should think so," I respond. I have not told her of my encounter with Tomasso, better not to share that with her. "It seems to me that with Mary dead, that should be the end of the thing, and I ought to have my money that much sooner."

She tries to calm me. "It's not quite that simple. The trust gave Mary the power to direct who got her interest in it after her death. That interest really includes the right to demand the entire trust under certain circumstances, mostly if you hadn't been thawed in a very long time. Well, it seems that Mary's will gave all her rights to Peter Dwyer, her husband. He used to be a lawyer, you know. And he intends to litigate your right to the trust."

"What does that mean?" I find myself getting angrier.

"It means we have a lawsuit on our hands," she says. "It means things won't be quite as simple as we thought at first. Dwyer is apparently claiming that since you were declared legally dead in 1979, and inheritance taxes were paid on your estate at that time, then for purposes of the law your rights to the trust should have terminated in 1979. Put at its most basic, he seems to be arguing that you are attempting to inherit from yourself and the law clearly prohibits that. No man can be his own heir."

My anger turns to fear. Janet is taking this

thing seriously, and I am becoming concerned. "What are his chances?" I ask. "How risky is this thing?"

"You never know how a judge is going to rule," she says. "You never know. Personally, I think we have a much better chance. Dwyer is a greedy old man. He looked after Mary for years, hoping to inherit the fortune. Now, he feels it has been snatched away from him at the very moment it was his. He is vindictive, angry, frustrated. But from a legal point of view, I don't think he has a good case. I think we will win."

I read the new affidavit, study it carefully on the shade screen. I have a few questions about the legal jargon. Once Janet has satisfied me on these, I take the stylus and sign the film. I've done it before, so I feel like a pro. I even remember my number. I'm starting to enjoy the year 2008.

XII

New York/March 5, 2008/9:15 P.M.

"Many of our concepts, our idea patterns, we call them, have changed from the last century," says Janet. "We are open to a diversity in a way in which your time was not, in a way unlike that of any previous time."

We are sitting on the lounging cushions in Janet's apartment, sipping fresh bottled water from the small glassine snifters. Mood vibrations and music are playing softly on the selectron.

My mind has turned to romance, and marriage. I ask Janet what her feelings are about romance. The response surprises and disappoints me. She explains that the concept of romance has become unfashionable.

"I suppose we feel toward romance the way people in your day felt toward vampires or witches," she says. "Romantic love is looked upon as a curious old fashioned idea. You still don't believe the world is flat, do you?"

"What about passion?" I say. I am trying to defend the flat world. "Don't you believe in the idea of two people in love, deeply in love, for whom nothing else matters but that love?"

"In old movies, yes, and in most of the nineteenth century operas. Otherwise, I'm afraid I can't subscribe to its reality."

I don't know how to respond. I no longer belong to Leland Anderson's generation. The museum re-creations of the Retrieved Association aren't really for me. I want to live in the here and now. I want to belong to Janet's age, but there is such a gulf in outlook and attitudes. I don't know if it can be bridged.

At the same time, I find myself attracted to her. It is a romantic attraction, and she has just characterized that as old fashioned, as something to be equated with a flat world or vampires. There is a physical attraction, but it is more than that. She is an exciting person. I find her exciting to be with. I enjoy relying on her. I appreciate her concern and desire to help me with the adjustments of my new life.

Her attitude, the society's attitude, toward marriage, makes even less sense to me. She explains that marriage has become a housing function. People marry in order to share housing.

168

When one spouse or the other finds the arrangements no longer convenient, the marriage is terminated by the filing of a Divorce Notice in the local government office.

"You mean," I say, "that if I get tired of living in that monster hotel and the Retrieved Association can't find me a seven foot bed, I could just marry you and move in here?"

She smiles. "Sure," she says.

I feel a rush of excitement. She continues, "I've already been married twice. First time it was to a guy who had a really swell apartment on the 323rd floor of the Skyview Towers. That marriage lasted two leases. Then the apartment really needed to be painted, and neither of us wanted to stay through the mess, so we both moved. It was a nice relationship, but two leases were really enough." She laughs. "My second marriage was to a fellow in the office. We both wanted to live near the office, so we shared the rent on a nice place just across the Mall. When he left the firm, we dissolved the marriage. The last two years, I've been living here, alone."

I remain excited. The prospect of using early twenty-first century processes to achieve my mid-twentieth century desires fascinates me. I pursue the point. "And you mean if I asked you, you'd marry me?"

"I already said sure."

Her response puzzles me. There is impatience in her voice, as if I am nagging at the subject. I don't understand her attitude. Finally, I ask, "But what's to distinguish marriage from

169

more casual relationships?"

"Very little," answers Janet. "It's really different ways of looking at the same thing. It's all to do with what I said before. We are open to a diversity of possibilities. We make no demand that those possibilities exhibit internal consistencies."

I try to swallow the reasoning, to clear myself for the final capture of the prey. But the swallow sticks in my throat. I hear myself sputtering, "But, but, but . . . . It doesn't make any sense. The government seems to exhibit so many controls, the need to register everywhere, the use of special numbers, all that, and yet in this area there is such freedom and openness."

"Oh, Dennis," she says, fixing my eyes. "Why must things make sense? Your world had its set of paradoxes and confusions. Our world has another set. If you're going to live in our world, you'll just have to adjust to it."

"Then marry me," I say, interrupting her as she pauses for breath.

Janet laughs and looks away. "I've already accepted your offer twice," she says. "I think if you repeat it once more, I may start to doubt your intentions."

"Let's do it now," I say. I get up from the cushion, expectantly, ready to snap up my jumpsuit and leave.

"It's too late," says Janet. "The administrative office closes at eight. But if you're still insistent in the morning, we can go over and get government clearance."

I sit again on the cushion. "That's just what I can't fathom," I say. "Why all the red tape, why all the government involvement, if there is really no significance to marriage, if people can live together without getting into trouble and without benefit of state sanctioned licenses?"

"I suppose I have been a little simplistic," says Janet. She finishes the water in her glass and pours another few drops from the bottle. Then she says, "You see, Dennis, something does turn on marriage, on the state sanctioned license: the right to have children. The laws are fairly strict in that area. I won't go into the punishment for out-of-wedlock children, but it's considered a pretty terrible crime. Marriage gives one the right to apply for a child license. In our case, of course, it really doesn't make any difference. Since I'm a professional, I wouldn't be having children. Still, that's the difference."

"And you mean that the government decides who can have children, and when?" I ask, incredulous.

"But of course, Dennis. Does that surprise you?" asks Janet. And the look she gives me tells me that she can't really fathom my surprise.

XIII

New York/March 12, 2008/11:50 P.M.

I have arranged my visit to the Retrieved Association for lunchtime. It is unconscious. Perhaps I find security in those horrible fake hamburgers. They at least have a look which reminds me of the food I used to enjoy.

I wait patiently in the reception area for Poore. There's a new magazine, a 1974 issue of "New York." I enjoy its topicality. I haven't gotten far into the magazine, when Poore is there to escort me away.

In his office, I ask, "Any success with my request for a standard size bed?"

"We're still looking. That's not an easy one

to fill. At one point the government declared long mattresses a health hazard and they were all confiscated, for the scrap metal content. So there are very few around. I've made some discrete inquiries, but so far, no luck."

"You'll keep looking?"

"We'll exhaust every source."

He seems sincere, anxious to help. I thank him. I smell the aroma of the grilling burgers in the snack shop down the corridor. It makes me hungry. I find myself salivating.

"You know," says Poore, "annual elections for the 1970s Association will be held next week. I'd like to put your name up for the Board. How do you feel about that?"

I am concentrating on the smells of food, smells I haven't known for so long. I bring myself back to his question, "What do I have to do, as a member of the Board?" I ask.

"Not too many responsibilities," he says. "There are monthly Board meetings. The Board supervises the museum and the services we perform for the members. It's like any other charitable-Board."

"Well, as long as I'm not expected to do more than attend meetings and know what's going on, I'll do it," I say. "But, if there's any more work, you'll do it!"

Poore laughs. "I do anyway," he says.

The smell of the grill is driving me crazy. "Let me buy you some lunch," I say finally.

"Sure, thanks," responds Poore.

I find myself wolfing down two of the

jumbo hamburger sandwiches, complete with all the "trimmings." Tastes and textures send my mouth into ecstasy. It's as if I have been without water for weeks and have just found the oasis.

Over lunch Poore asks about my housing situation. I explain that I have married Janet and we are living in her apartment, but looking for a new one. He gives me the name of a government agent who specializes in apartments for Retrieveds from the 1970s and early 1980s.

After lunch I call the agent. He suggests that I meet him at the Park Plaza, a new complex built on the air rights over Central Park.

The people mover takes me almost to the door. The approach is a short path through the park. Then there are the high speed elevators to the lobby platform, 200 feet above ground. There the stilts of the building and the park are visible through the glass floored lobby.

I meet Mr. Archer, the agent, at the appointed time.

"I think you'll like Park Plaza," he says, "the location is perfect and it has all the latest conveniences."

He takes me to something he calls the perfect apartment for me, on the 97th floor. The exterior elevator provides a pleasant view of the park and the surrounding towers as we go up. But the speed of the elevator forms a knot in my stomach.

When we arrive, I find the apartment claustrophobic. The lounging room has what I have discovered are the standard measurements for lounging rooms. It is nine by twelve, but it looks smaller. The food assembly closet is keyed in to a central computer so it is kept constantly stocked in up to 24 different varieties of prepared food-stuffs. It is small but adequate. The eating bar will serve two, perhaps three with difficulty.

Behind the lounging room are the two small sleeping rooms. I look at the dimensions of these and wonder again if I could fit a standard bed in the small rooms, if one could be found.

Off the lounging room is a small terrace, enclosed in mesh grid, to protect against vertigo problems.

In all it is a tiny apartment, but it fits the style of the day. Space is at a premium. Living space has been reduced to a minimum, to all that is needed to be workable. The rent is eight seventy-five a month, and Mr. Archer discreetly suggests that a month's rent as a gift to the building manager might be required to save the apartment for us. Graft and corruption. Always graft and corruption.

I refuse to make a commitment. I want Janet to see it first. I promise to get her over as soon as possible.

"It better be today, or the apartment might not be left," says Mr. Archer, dismissing me. So much for apartments. So much for the good life in the year 2008.

XIV

New York/March 14, 2008/9:46 A.M.

We arrive at the courthouse early. Janet is nervous. It is her big case. But for her it's a job; for me a fortune hangs in the balance.

We walk up the marble steps, into the enormous foyer, with its imposing marble staircase. Ceilings are covered in gilt, all the trappings of law and government.

The ancient elevator takes us up to the fifth floor. Then it is a short walk to the courtroom, a large dark panelled chamber. When we arrive, Anderson is already there. This upsets Janet; she had hoped to arrive before the old man. It's a form of one-upmanship prevalent in the firm. Anderson is old and wise, and he is there first.

Anderson has chosen a large mahogany chair for himself. He offers another to Janet. I am told that I must sit in the back, on a straight chair. Comfort is reserved for the lawyers. The litigants, it seems, are second class citizens.

I recognize Peter Dwyer at the other counsel table. He is his own lawyer. I watch him stare at me and I wonder at his thoughts. Time has etched his face, but it can still be identified as the same face that led the Tomasso prosecution, so long ago.

Suddenly there is a loud bang on an exterior door. An usher shouts, "All rise," and the door swings open. I follow the lead of Anderson and Janet, and stand in place as the black-robed judge enters.

The usher mumbled a brief invocation. The only thing that is audible is the closing phrase, "The Honorable Charles J. O'Hare presiding." The judge has been identified.

In another moment, the usher calls our case, "In the Matter of the Dennis Minton Trust." I am ready to jump up and say, "Here, your honor," but I restrain myself. I have legal representation. They will do what is necessary.

Anderson introduces himself and Janet to the court. He whispers and I can barely hear him. I wonder if he is up to making this argument. Is he doing it just for vanity, or for old times sake, or for what?

Anderson begins his argument. His voice is

so low I cannot hear it. I change seats, moving up closer to the front of the room. Still, no use. I hear only a drone and an occasional wheeze. I am disturbed. I find myself counting the wooden squares in the ceiling, analyzing the bas relief of the wooden panels, counting the spindles in the balustrade around the balcony.

The room is old. Late nineteenth century, I would guess. It has many delights for the eye. But I am concerned about my case and the fact that my lawyer speaks so softly I can't even hear him. I hope the judge can hear him.

I focus on Dwyer. He is busy jotting notes. Where he sits he must be able to hear Anderson, and he must think Anderson is saying things that require response. There is some consolation to that.

Summoning all my attention, I hear the old man's voice bouncing weakly off the ceiling. It seems to echo against the marble floor. He coughs. I hear a stirring demand by Anderson for vindication of his client's right, my rights. It sounds good, and it is over. Too soon, too soon.

Now it is Dwyer's turn. He rises, walks to the lectern deliberately and begins with the ancient words of ritual, *May it please the Court.*

As he speaks the ritual formula, he seems to bow ever so slightly, perhaps it is nothing more than a nod, but something makes it look like an act of entreaty. Behind the high wooden dais, the bench of the court, I see Judge O'Hare. He seems unmoved by entreaty.

Dwyer tells the story from the beginning. He

explains to the judge that I was dying from Hays Syndrome, that I turned to freezing as a last resort, in the hope that one day I might be thawed and cured. He explains how I put virtually all of my wealth into the trust, the subject matter of this litigation, on the day before my freezing at Cryo Genius.

Dwyer's telling of the story puts special emphasis on the period while I was frozen. He describes in some detail the proceedings of 1979 during which I was legally declared dead. He reminds the court that at that time a substantial inheritance tax had been paid on my estate.

Dwyer bangs his hand against the lectern. He argues that irrespective of any other facts, the earlier legal proceedings should bar me from recovering the balance of the trust.

Finally he deals with the relevance of an ancient legal doctrine, the Rule Against Perpetuities, which apparently prohibits trusts from continuing for an indefinite length of time. Speaking slowly, so that I can hear him well, he says, "At the time Dennis Minton was frozen, no one could know how long he would remain in that state, no one could know how long it would be before Hays Syndrome would be cured. He might have been frozen for hundreds of years, even thousands of years. There was no limit. Generations might have passed, and Minton might still have been frozen. With all respect to the Honorable Court, I submit that this is a violation of the Rule Against Perpetuities. I submit that any trust which is to continue until a cure for a particular disease has been found, must clearly be in violation of the Rule."

There is a pause. Dwyer drinks from the glass of water on the lectern. I see the arm of the black robe sweeping back and forth over a page of yellow paper. The Judge is taking notes. It looks like Dwyer has made a point which the judge has bought.

Dwyer continues. His voice sounds more confident. "As your Honor is no doubt aware, the remedy when a trust violates the Rule Against Perpetuities is to invalidate those portions of the trust which violate the Rule, and to permit the other trust provisions to stand. Here, the life income interest to Mary Minton Dwyer was proper. The provision permitting Mrs. Dwyer to direct where the principal was to go on her death was also proper. The only provision that was improper was the one requiring that the principal vest in Minton after his thawing, since that could be hundreds of years from now. Under the circumstances, the balance of the trust must belong to the Estate of Mary Minton Dwyer."

Dwyer has finished his argument. He slowly releases his grasp on the lectern. He looks confident. I have listened and even I have been swayed by his rhetoric. I watch him walk the few steps back to his council table. He has a firm step.

The air in the room is electric. The silence amplifies the rustling at the other table. Janet and Anderson huddle together. They whisper. I restrain my desire to join the huddle.

In a moment Janet has moved to the lectern. "If it please your Honor," she says, "and with Mr.

181

Dwyer's indulgence, I will respond on behalf of the petitioner, Mr. Minton, since Mr. Anderson is indisposed."

I look over to the counsel table. Anderson is white. His mouth hangs open sloppily. I am concerned for the old man, but also uncertain that Janet can handle the case alone, can respond to Dwyer's eloquence.

The judge asks Dwyer if he objects. "Certainly not, your Honor," he responds. No one asks me if I object, if I want more time to find a lawyer who isn't an enfeebled old man or my wife.

Janet speaks quickly. Her words slur and she seems to race through her thoughts as if she is rushing to catch the last train to some distant suburb. But her argument sounds good.

"Your Honor," she says, "we can't let a legal fiction obscure a real fact. We must remember it was a legal fiction, and nothing more, which resulted in the declaration in 1979 that Minton was a dead man. In fact he wasn't a dead man, he was only frozen. In fact, Minton was thawed, and cured, and he has met the terms of the trust, and he is entitled to have the principal vest in him."

She pauses to glance down at her notes. There must be scribblings on a yellow legal pad.

She continues, "The Rule Against Perpetuities is a false issue, thrown up by Mr. Dwyer to becloud the real facts. The truth about the Rule Against Perpetuities is that it never cuts down a trust which will vest during the lives of people in being at its inception. Minton was a life in being at the inception of this trust. He is still alive, and entitled to the trust. Even if it could be said that by some stretch of the imagination, under some fantastic circumstances we might imagine, that this trust might go on too long, the fact is that it has not gone on too long. And the Rule Against Perpetuities has nothing to do with this case."

She speaks for no more than five minutes, but her delivery is rapid fire. The judge takes many notes. It looks like a good sign.

Janet sits. The electric silence fills the room again. The judge continues to take notes. The scrawl of his pen is amplified across the room. There is a cough from the back. The judge looks up. He eyes counsel at the two tables. Finally he announces, "Decision reserved, submit briefs in fourteen days."

He has refused to rule on the question solely on the basis of the oral argument. He has asked for written memoranda of law from both sides. It is not a surprise, but it will mean more work for Janet.

I go forward to congratulate her on her argument, and to see about Anderson. He is very pale. "Do you need a doctor, Lee?" I ask.

"No, I'll be fine, I'll be fine," he says. Then nodding at Janet, he adds, "Didn't she do a great job, there?"

I congratulate her, and ask what the reserved decision means.

"It means time," she says. "It means time. Under the stipulation by which the matter was heard, the Trustees are under an obligation to continue to make payments to Dwyer, as Mary's beneficiary until the matter is decided by th court. We may have a long time ahead of us It could take a month, maybe six weeks fo O'Hare's initial decision, six weeks for reargu ment, six months for appeal to Special Term an another six months for appeal to the Appeal Court. Even if the judicial mills grind at their fas est, it may be more than a year before we have final result."

It seems so long, so long to have these unce tainties, to have this damn thing hanging over m head. The expectations of the day in court hav suddenly been dashed. As we leave the ornat court room, the eagle perched over the door look like a vulture, too much like a vulture.

XV

New York/March 22, 2008/8:23 A.M.

"Janet," I say. She is almost to the door; my call brings her back. "Janet, I'd like to help."

"What do you mean?" She is impatient to leave. I can see her whole body straining to carry her away to the office.

"Well, you go off to the office every morning, and I do nothing. And the last week especially, you've been working so hard, such long hours, and I know it's on the legal papers on my case. Isn't there anything I can do?"

I find I am pleading to be useful, to have some purpose to my own existence, some dignity which is mine alone.

Janet comes over to the lounging cushion. The tension has left her body and she relaxes in the cushion. She touches my hand. "That's sweet of you, Dennis, very sweet of you." It is an act affection, an act of warmth that almost seems o of place in this cold world. "Let me think," s says, "what is there that you could do?"

I am anxious, hopeful. "I'll do anything," say, "research the law, anything."

"No," responds Janet, "legal research we leave to the lawyers. But there is something, y there is something. You can come down to the fice with me and sort the old files. We have dra ers and drawers of files on you. You can so them, get me the relevant ones."

"Okay, sure."

We are off together, down the elevator the people mover and along the people mover the office. It's an easy trip.

At the office, Janet directs me to a sm room; she goes to the library. The room I am l in is windowless. Along one side are dozens faded, tattered manila envelopes. They awe n

For a few minutes I am almost afraid to a proach the piles of documents, afraid of drowni in them.

Finally, I start picking at them. I open or It is a legal file, an old legal file from a dea made in 1965. I look through it; I remember t deal, an apartment complex in Maryland. made a lot of money. Thumbing the old papers enjoyable. Memories flood back. But they are useful memories. Soon I must close the file a ut it to one side.

I try another. It's a file from my office, an ld correspondence file, blue copies of letters I ent, all in chronological order, for some future istorian, for me. It is all interesting, even more ngaging than the first file. The letters appear at andom and content ranges from trivial to pround. But it deals with the wrong period, a small lice of 1972. Nothing of use here.

Slowly I pick another file. I try to make the hoice with care; but even so it is a blind lottery. ach file engages my attention at least for ten or ifteen minutes, even though it doesn't further ly case.

Time passes quickly. Before long I find huner gnawing at my stomach. And I am exhausted y the emotional trip, by the recollections reawaened. I have gone through many files, but none et are helpful. They have been placed in this oom at random. Each has a little piece of me, a ttle piece of my life. Each is part of my own jigaw-puzzle. But putting it together could take ears. I'm not sure I'm up to the job.

I seek out Janet and find her behind the omputer printout terminal in a cubicle in the lirary. She is busy with her research, narrowing he scope of the computer selected cases.

"Ready for lunch?" I ask. But she is too eeply into the work. She motions me to go on lone.

Without thought I find myself leaving the uilding, and taking the people mover to the Rerieved Association Museum, to the one real haven I know.

In the snack shop I munch at my hamburger and think about the files, about the digging that i required. Another mind is needed, someone who can open up those envelopes without ripping open something inside himself each time. I realize can't go back. I'll have to give Janet some excuse when she gets home this evening.

XVI

New York/April 21, 2008/8:41 A.M.

"O'Hare ruled against us!" Janet has looked up from her egg substitute flakes in the plastic cup to give me the news.

I stand at the doorway of the food assembly area. I have been hit in the stomach, in the groin. "Oh my God!" I respond. There are no words, there are no thoughts, only dumb fear. The pyramid is dissolving into the sand.

I grasp forward. "Did you get a copy of the decision?" I want to know what the judge said, how he reached his decision, what hope there is, what chance of overturning it. Even as I ask the question and I walk over to the egg substitute dispenser, other tracks become active in my mind.

I find myself thinking of Janet and our relationship. I am so insecure about it. I'm afraid that if my fortune is lost, she, too, may be lost. I watch for a sign, a hint, a suggestion that her feelings have changed, that she is about to pack up and leave.

I think also of old Anderson. He was once such a towering figure. Now he seems impotent, all his legal constructions no more than castles in the sand washed away by the tides.

And for reasons I do not altogether understand, I am afraid, deeply afraid.

Janet is talking. She breaks my train of thought with the response to my question to her. "No, Dennis," she says, "I don't have a copy of the decision. I got the news in a photophone message from the office, it was waiting when I got up. They have promised a full reproduction of the decision by the time I get to the office." She wipes a few flakes from the side of her mouth and continues, "Now, don't get upset, Dennis. This is nothing to get upset about. O'Hare is a feebleminded dolt. I didn't like the idea of appearing before him, but we had no choice. Don't worry dear. I'm sure we can get this one reversed on appeal."

She sounds reassuring, but I am not reassured. My mind has set in the prospect of the worst. I take a cup of the green flakes and sit down on the stool next to Janet. I let my jumpsuit brush against hers, just to remind her of our commitment to each other. Then I ask, "Jan, baby, *what if*? I mean we never really faced this, we've never talked about it. What if I lose?"

She stiffens. She moves away ever so slightly. The movement is barely perceptible, but I perceive it. And I know the answer. No matter what she says in response, her body has spoken, and I understand rather more than I want to, and I am not hungry at all.

We talk for a while. She keeps assuring me that we will win in the appeals court. She sounds sure of herself, but I am not convinced. The uneasiness does not leave me until she has left for the office.

Then, alone in the apartment, I am able to put the equation together very simply. I understand that if the case is lost, my fortune will be, too. That doesn't really disturb me. Ken Poore has indicated that any time I want it there's a job for me at the Retrieved Museum. I am the youngest living 20th century man, and as such I could certainly support myself well lecturing on life in the mid-twentieth century.

No, the loss of the fortune has other implications. It means the loss of Janet, this ingratiating person to whom I am married. I am fascinated by her. The prospect of losing her overwhelms me. I wish I could renounce these old fashioned notions of romance, but I can't, and I feel that I love her.

So the problem is understood. Only a solution remains to be found. I will seek out peace at the Retrieved Museum. Maybe there I will find a solution.

XVII

New York/April 21, 2008/10:20 A.M.

I am sitting on the sofa, watching old quiz shows. 1972 television fare is featured this week. The pictures deaden the mind. They are an antidote to pain. They provide quiet, but no concentration.

The telephone rings. I pick it up.

"Mr. Minton," the receptionist says, "there's a gentleman to see you, a government gentleman, a Mr. Tomasso."

Tomasso? What is he after me for this time? I am suspicious. But I have no choice. I tell her to send him into the 1970s living room.

I switch off the television with regret, and

turn to see Tomasso in his bulging green jumpsuit. He offers a greeting and says, "Well, I come to wish you a Happy Birthday, if you know what I mean."

"No," I respond. "I don't know what you mean." It's not my birthday, and I haven't the vaguest notion what he is talking about.

"Well, you see, it's like this," continues Tomasso, taking possession of the large armchair in the center of the room, as if to exert his dominion over the entire room. "I came to congratulate you on your victory in the courts."

"You've picked the wrong man," I say, "I lost in the courts. The decision only just came out today. Go visit Mr. Dwyer if you're going to offer congratulations."

"Come, come, Dennis," says the other. "This is just the first round. I know what happened with O'Hare. But that can be fixed. It all can be *fixed*. There are going to be appeals here, lots of appeals. Tony Tomasso's the guy to fix it for you."

I feel a knot forming in my stomach. The cold beads of perspiration appear just below my brow. I feel ill, but stifle the revulsion and ask, "How much?"

"Well, let's see," says Tomasso, relaxing into the chair. "There'll be a reargument in front of O'Hare, but I suppose we ought to give up on him. You know how extravagant he is. He really lives beyond his means. The people we have to deal with are the three boobs on the appellate court, and I suppose we can get by with two of the three on the court of appeals. And then of course there's me. I don't work for nothing. And there are a few of my friends." He pauses to total the requirements slowly, with the aid of the fingers of both hands. Then he says, "Look, Dennis, I think I can get you a nice wrapped up deal for three million."

I can't believe what I have heard. "What?" I say in exclamation.

Tomasso repeats the analysis, more slowly, going more deeply into the demands of each of the officials. The total does indeed come to just under three million dollars. He continues, "Look, Dennis, we know you can't pay right now, things are tied up as long as the litigation continues. I don't have any problems about that, but we do need our protection, if you know what I mean. So we'll take your I.O.U.s."

It is too much for me. I look around the room for witnesses. There are none. I want to yell for the police, but I stifle the impulse. Tomasso is the police. He already has my confession to Mary's murder. He is becoming my evil genius.

Quietly I ask, "What if I refuse?"

"Dennis," he responds, "you ain't going to do that. You see this way you get six million bucks, the other way, you don't get nothing."

"I see," I say, but it is merely a figure of speech.

Tomasso continues, "It just happens that I have them I.O.U.s right here. So, if you'd like to sign them, I can get going." Tomasso produces a micro-mini-fiche stylus and a strip of film from

195

his pocket. He picks himself up out of the chair and brings them over to me.

I focus on the stylus, and then on Tomasso. "I don't have a choice, do I?" I ask.

"Sure you have a choice," says Tomasso, patting me on the back. "Nothing says you got to win the lawsuit. Nothing says you got to get that money. You have to sign only if you want to win. And anyway, you don't pay nothing until you get the money. It looks to me like a great deal for you. And the rest of us, well, we're in the business, too, you know."

I think of Janet's reaction to the loss in O'Hare's court, of the uncertainty of the appeals which lie ahead. Corruption revolts me, but certainty, assurances have a fascination I cannot resist. I sign the notes secured by my interest in the Minton trust and payable on demand.

Tomasso leaves quickly. I am alone again in the 1970s.

XVIII

New York/April 21, 2008/3:20 P.M.

There is a message on the photophone when
return to the apartment from the museum. It is
rom Dwyer. He wants to see me. Strange.

I dial him back. "This is Dennis Minton," I
ay. "You called me."

"Yes," comes the answer, "I'd like to talk to
ou, privately, as soon as possible. Could I come
ver now?"

"Surely." And I switch off.

In twenty minutes Dwyer is announced on
he building intercom, and in another five, he
ings the bell.

"Come in," I say. It is clear he has come to

discuss the lawsuit, but I haven't had time to put my mind in order, to consider the possibilities, to decide on alternatives.

There is a moment of awkwardness. I sense him staring at me, as he did in court. I decide to deal with the issue. "People who knew me in the old days are struck by how little I've changed," I say, "but of course that really shouldn't be so surprising. After all, I was in a state of suspended animation for thirty years."

"Still, it's uncanny," says Dwyer, almost to himself, "It's as if the past, my own past, is staring me in the face."

"I'm sorry."

"Oh, no. It's not your fault."

Dwyer settles himself in a lounging cushion. He says, "Let me come right to the point. I've read O'Hare's opinion, and I think it's a good opinion. Judicious, sound. But I think the time has come to settle this matter. I know this litigation has been a strain on me, and I'm sure it must also be a strain on you. I'm willing to split it down the middle, and withdraw my objections to the termination of the trust."

I cross to the cabinet where I keep the bottled water. "That's a very interesting offer," I say and then, remembering to be polite, I add, "Can I offer you some water?"

"No thanks," responds Dwyer. He is all business, and makes that clear.

I open the bottle and pour an ounce into the small glass. I pretend to be deeply engrossed in the activity. But I am really assessing this offer

198

and its relationship with the discussion I had with Tomasso this morning at the Retrieved Association. I sip the water and quietly say, "Just because one feeble-minded judge wrote an aberration of a decision, that's not going to give you half of my trust, Mr. Dwyer. Now make me a serious offer."

I can't say why I have chosen this route. It is a sham. There is nothing I will agree to. I have made my deal already with Tony, and there is no renegging on that. But Dwyer offers sport, excitement, the thrill of poker. I can't resist.

"I'll take three million five," says Dwyer, without changing his position on the lounging cushion.

I sip some more water. The expert poker player must draw his opponent out, draw him out to the fullest before administering the *coup de grace*. I toy with his new bid. I let a long time pass while I sip at the water and play with my glass. I let the room grow silent enough so that I can measure Dwyer's breathing.

Then, I say, "No, three million five is too much. I can't do it. It just doesn't sound right." I smile. It is the quiet smile of an accomplished poker player fielding a winning hand.

Dwyer squirms. He changes his position on the cushion and clenches the nail on his left thumb in his teeth.

"Three million, and I can't take a penny less," he says.

I think it strange. Dwyer has now offered me the same deal I bought from Tomasso this morning. I long for escape. There is none.

Dwyer continues, pleading, "Mr. Minton, Judge O'Hare has just ruled in my favor in this matter. I would have thought that if there were serious settlement negotiations, I would be getting the lion's share of the trust. But I'm an old man. I'm willing to settle. I'm willing to take a third, and be done with it."

I walk to the window and look out at the towers. Then I turn to Dwyer and say, "O'Hare's decision is going to be reversed. Everyone knows that. If you want to settle, you have to make me an offer which realistically reflects the fact that this is my money, my wealth, and my lawyers are going to save it all for me."

"It's not quite like that," he responds. I have awakened the sleeping lawyer in him. "What you did in 1978 was establish a trust, and then the money stopped being yours and it belonged to the trust. And from then on, the disposition of the money must be governed by the terms of that trust. I think that Mary's estate is entitled to that trust now. It's a matter of principle, but I'm willing to give it up, to get this thing settled."

He pauses. He looks old, older than he did in the court room. The case has taken a toll on him already. He is pleading, pleading for mercy, for an end to the ordeal.

"Look, Minton," he says, "you drive a hard bargain. I'm an old man; my needs aren't very great. I think I'm entitled to half this trust, but I'll trade the uncertainties, the fears of this litigation, for two million five. That's it. I can't go any

200

lower."

I can't help wondering what my response would have been had I not met Tomasso at the museum. This sounds like the solution, but it is barred, barred by Tomasso's scheming and the I.O.U.s in the pocket of his green jumpsuit.

The charade is over. Finally I say, "No, Mr. Dwyer, I can't be bought off."

"You're a fool," responds the other. "Don't you see what you're doing. This litigation is going to kill me. It may kill you, too. Can't you stop? Can't you get off my back?"

The outburst is sad, poignant. But there is nothing left, no possibilities. Quietly, I say, "I don't think we have anything left to talk about."

And Dwyer storms out of the apartment.

XIX

New York/August 18, 2008/2:40 P.M.

I find security again in the eighth floor reception room. It is familiar. I have been here so
many times before, and it summons so carefully
my memories of the 1970s. I enjoy sitting in a
heavy chair and thumbing the old magazines
while I wait for Ken Poore. Each visit, it seems,
there is a new batch of 1970s issues, some quite
exciting. And the wait is never long enough; there
is never enough time to digest this first experience
of the museum fully.

This time Poore is particularly bubbly as he
escorts me into his small office. "You don't know
how pleased the administrative office is," he says,

"that you agreed to give this lecture series." Lowering his voice to a more confidential tone, he adds, "You're considered a real plum."

I feel uncomfortable. "As I told you," I say, "I'm not doing it because I want to. Frankly, since the judge ruled against me in my lawsuit, I really need the money. We've been trying to live on Janet's income, but we just can't, so I thought this would help."

Poore is sympathetic. "How is the lawsuit going?"

"Janet argued the appeal last week. We're waiting for a decision. It may be awhile. I'm hopeful, but one never can tell how a court will decide."

He nods in agreement, then returns to the subject of my lecture. "Well, whatever your reason," he says, "we're all sure you're going to be a tremendous success and a great asset for the oral history program."

"Thank you," I say, relaxing slightly into the chair. "That's really what I wanted to talk to you about." I open the large portfolio I have had tucked under my arm. I fumble through and take out some papers. "Ken," I say, "I'm disturbed by what happened with my first three lectures. I submitted them to the Editorial Board, like you said I should, and they've come back all marked up. I brought them along so you could take a look at them yourself." As I speak, I pass the papers across the desk, for Poore's review.

I watch closely while Poore's eyes dart across the pages. He nods significantly or frowns, by turns. Finally he is finished; he looks up at me and there is an embarrassed smile on his face. "Well, sir," he says, "that's the Editorial Board for you."

The response doesn't satisfy me. I find the smile only succeeds in getting me angry. "Ken," I say, "that's censorship. They're not letting me tell it my way, the way it was. They've cut out all references to civil liberties, to independence. They're rewriting history, and they want me to shill for them."

The smile disappears from Poore's face. "I know how you feel," he says, "but you have to realize that in dealing with the past there has to be distillation. Someone has to be responsible for the emphasis, the themes, the contexts of any set of historical events. The Editorial Board serves that function here. You're just being asked to make a few changes in your lectures to conform to prevailing theories about the history of the middle of the twentieth century."

"It's dishonest," I respond. I am still angry. "It's a fraud. Do you think I'm some puppet they can make mouth whatever they want?"

"No," explains Poore. "What the Editorial Board is really saying is that since you lived during the period you were too close to it to appreciate what was really going on. You can talk about your experiences, but when it comes to drawing broad historical conclusions, that has to be left to the people who know, the professionals who have studied the period dispassionately." He pauses, seeming to wait for some change in my expression. When there is none, he adds, "Look, you and I really lived through those times, and we know how much better things are now, so we've got to go along."

"I wouldn't do it if I didn't need the money."

"Oh, you're going to be a great success," says Poore. "There's been a lot of interest in your lectures. I expect the series will be a sellout." He takes a sheaf of publicity material from the table at the side of his desk and reviews various items with me. The publicity looks good; very good. It reduces my anger.

When he is finished I find myself asking again about my old request. "Anything new on the bed situation?"

"Still looking," he responds, "still looking."

The meeting is over. As I am leaving the office, Poore calls, "By the way, in doing a computer check on Janet we discovered a cute coincidence. Her grandfather was also named Dennis Minton."

XX

New York/August 18, 2008/3:30 P.M.

The trip back to the apartment is interminable. I try to will the people mover to speed, but it is no use. Its pace seems slower than ever.

Finally I am there. I go directly to that old picture album, the one I have thumbed through casually a few times before. The early pictures in that album of Janet's have always had a special meaning for me, but I have never recognized their meaning until now. I look at them and I know I have seen them before, long before meeting Janet.

As I flip page after page, my certainty increases. Suddenly an image jumps out at me from the page. It is me. There I am standing in front of

207

a house, a young man of 21. And with me are two others, my first wife, Irene, and our infant daughter, Barbara. I don't have to puzzle over the photograph long. It is the key, the key to Poore's cute coincidence. *Janet's grandfather was named Dennis Minton. I am Janet's grandfather.*

I close the album. I remember that Janet said her mother, Barbara, lived in a condominium in the Amazon valley. We received occasional letters from her, but she hasn't visited New York in years. That woman, Janet's mother, my own mother-in-law, is also my daughter.

For the first time I understand something about my attraction to Janet which I have never appreciated before. There is something about her reminiscent of Irene, or maybe even of myself. An elusive quality, but it is there, it is real.

I am frightened, frightened by the emotional context, and also by the legal implications. I am afraid of this authoritarian government. I have seen its censorship at work. I know that the legal code provides the most terrible of penalties for insignificant infractions; I hate to think what the punishment is for marrying one's own granddaughter. It must be horrible.

My first thought is to conceal it from Janet. She is upset about the case, worried about the appeal and has seemed particularly tense recently. I am concerned that this revelation about our relationship could upset her even further.

But the thing gnaws at me. There is no getting away from it. It is central. I can't avoid it. To keep it from her would be worse.

When Janet comes home I show her the pic-
re, the picture of me at 21. I explain that the
hers in the picture are my first wife and our
by daughter.

"Yes, and that baby is my mother, Barbara
iller," she says. "That means that you are my
andfather, at least biologically speaking."

She isn't revolted. Instead, she seems amused
the discovery. "Aren't you disturbed by this?"
sk.

"Why should I be?" she responds. "It could
ly create a problem if we were hoping to have
ildren, but of course we're not. Anyway, given
e facts, the government would never give us a
ild license, so it isn't really a problem at all."

I am still concerned, still surprised by her
sponse. "What about the laws?" I ask, "the
ws against marrying a near relation? Aren't we
olating those laws? Couldn't we get into trouble
out it?"

She laughs. It is the same laugh I have heard
many times before when I have applied mid-
ventieth century notions to the early twenty-
rst century. "Oh, those laws have all been re-
ealed," she explains. "I think the Retrieved As-
ciation was instrumental in getting the repeals.
ere have been a lot of father-daughter, mother-
n marriages among the Retrieved who end up in
e same age group as their children. There's no
oblem with it, so long as there are no offspring
the marriage."

"And you're not upset by the fact that I'm
ur grandfather?" I ask. I still can't comprehend

her attitude.

"No, not upset in the slightest," she says "But I do think we should write Mother about it Maybe now she'll decide to rouse herself from th Amazon and pay us a visit. She might enjoy meeting her own father as a person younger than sh is. She used to say that she never knew you at all since you and her mother were divorced when sh was so young. Well, now she's in her 50s, and yo are only 40. *She* could be *your* mother!"

And that seems the limit of Janet's interes in the problem of our biological relationship; it i a paradox and nothing more.

XXI

New York/September 4, 2008/12:30 P.M.

We are sitting in the snack shop at the Museum, Tomasso and me. We are munching at rubbery hamburgers, but I find I have no appetite.

"I can't understand it," I say. "I can't understand it. What happened? You were supposed to deliver that court, everything was fixed. What happened?"

"Don't get excited, Dennis," he says. "Don't get excited. Sometimes these things have to go this way at first, so it doesn't look fishy later on, if you know what I mean."

I can't stand that phrase of his. "No, I don't know what you mean," I say. "All I know is we had a deal. You were delivering me a verdict, first at the appellate court and then if we have to go all the way, at the court of appeals. But you see, if we had won here, maybe there wouldn't be a court of appeals. Maybe Dwyer would have called it quits." I am gesturing with half a hamburger, making wide arcs, pushing the soggy mess into his face.

"Look, Dennis, we lost. What can I say?" He shrugs and the green cloth of his jumpsuit stretches further out of shape. "All I can tell you is that we're going to win at the Court of Appeals. Sullivan and Metz, they're my buddies. They know all about this deal, all about it. No trouble with them."

"But that's only two judges. Aren't there three on that court?" I have put the hamburger down. It looks mean, ugly.

"Yeah, there are three, but all we need is two. Two votes wins. Anyway, it's cheaper to buy two, and I ain't so sure about the third guy. I ain't so sure."

"What about the others." I sip at the milk shake. It has coagulated.

"Good as golden," says Tomasso. "Good as golden. Sullivan, Metz, they're okay, they're on our side you can be sure of that. Nothing to worry about, Dennis. Nothing to worry about."

And yet I do. I do.

XXII

New York/February 7, 2009/8:38 A.M.

I hear a scream from the food assembly area, and, half dressed, rush to see the problem. My mind rushes past possibilities, an intruder, a mouse. In a moment I see Janet, standing by the counter, clutching a photophone message. Tears are streaming down her face.

"We've won," she gasps. "It's over; the case is over and we've won. The Court of Appeals decided for us. The trust is yours." I embrace her; hug her close to me. Even give her a kiss.

I am elated and only slightly surprised. Tomasso has come through, finally, and must be paid; but still there is a fortune, secure enough

213

for me.

I take the message from her hand and scan it. "Judge Wilner," it says, "rendered the decision granting the entire principal of the trust to Mr. Minton."

"What's this Judge Wilner?" I ask. "Who is he?"

The tears have stopped and her composure is returning. "Wilner?" she says. "He's one of the judges on the court, good legal mind."

"What about Sullivan," I say, "Sullivan and Metz?"

She is taking her egg substitute flakes from the dispenser. "Sullivan and Metz? Didn't I tell you about that accident? In October. I thought I had mentioned it to you. Two of the judges on the court were killed in a freak car accident. Most bizarre thing imaginable. Car swerved into a tree on a clear day. Both judges killed. That was Sullivan and Metz. Why do you ask about them?"

"So they didn't have anything to do with the decision on this case?" I say.

"No, nothing at all. We had to wait for the appointment of two new judges before we could even argue the case. It was a good bench. Good judicial minds. Why do you ask about Sullivan and Metz?"

I have no reply. There is none. But my mind percolates. It percolates for some time. Through breakfast, even after Janet has left for the office, I am still sitting at the counter, thinking. Putting the pieces together again and again and each time coming up with the same result.

I smell a double cross. I smell Tomasso a-bout to descend on me, to collect three million dollars for doing nothing. He never delivered the appellate court, and his two judges on the court of appeals were dead before the case was heard. We won on the merits, there's no question about that. Tomasso never reached the judges, never reached any of them.

My mind is determined; Tomasso will not share in my good fortune. It is not an act of cour-age, more one of desperation. I soon find myself sitting in the office of the Deputy Chief of the Interrogation Agents, telling my story.

"Yes, there is no question about it," I say, "he is one of the Retrieved. I don't know why he wants to hide it, but he and I were frozen at the same time at Hudson Bay in Canada."

"Why was he frozen?" asks the Agent.

"He was wanted for murder, the case was to be tried in White Ridge, New York, in September 1978. He was wanted for murder and he escaped, and he took me with him to Hudson Bay."

"Very interesting, but why didn't you come forward with the story sooner, as soon as you dis-covered the facts, my good man?"

"Officer," I explain. "I was scared. I still am scared. The man threatened me. He forced me to sign a statement implicating me in the murder of my wife, at a time when I was hundreds of miles away from here, being thawed. He warned me that if I ever exposed him, he would produce the confession and destroy me."

"And how come you're no longer afraid of

that, if you don't mind my asking?" says the officer. He puffs at a large pipe with a curved stem.

"Tomasso did more," I explain. "He forced me into a scheme to bribe judges, the judges deciding a lawsuit I was involved in. I discovered today that I won that suit, but not with Tomasso's help. The judges he had bribed were killed in a car accident. Now that I've won on the merits, I'm more confident. I want to see Tomasso get his. He doesn't frighten me as much anymore."

"It's a very serious crime," muses the officer. He is puffing away at the pipe. "Failure to answer a warrant is a capital offense under the Criminal Code of 2003. You realize that if what you say is true, then Tomasso could be sentenced to death?"

I sit very straight in the chair and say, "I understand. You check the records; you'll find that everything I've said is true, and the man is working for you, right here in this department."

"You can be sure, my good man," says the officer, "we will investigate this thoroughly, I say."

XXIII

New York/February 10, 2009/8:10 P.M.

We eat at home, something simple, soybean cakes and extruded broccoli. In the lounging room we watch the shade screen and listen to the sonophonic sound system.

Janet is quiet, particularly quiet. She has barely responded to my questions during dinner, and now, she sits silently, lost in thought.

The contrast from our two day celebration of the court victory is shocking. The smiles and laughter are gone. I am about to ask her what is bothering me when she looks at me and says, "Dennis, does the name Anthony Tomasso mean anything to you?"

I don't see the problem. "Yes," I say. "He's somebody from my past. I've seen him a few times over the last year. He's a government interrogation agent now, I believe. Why do you ask?" The knot is forming in my stomach. I start to worry that something has gone wrong, something about Tomasso, about the I.O.U.s, or the bribery or the confession to Mary's murder. Something.

She looks deeply at me. Her pale blue eyes are set off by black lashes. The eyes are watering, filling with tears, and brimming over.

"What's the matter?" I am scared.

"Tomasso was tried in connection with the things that went on at Cryo Genius, wasn't he?" she says, through the tears.

"Yes."

"And you were supposed to be a witness at the trial, weren't you?" she continues.

"Yes."

"And you left to be frozen at Hudson Bay before the trial was over, before you were even called to testify, didn't you?"

"Yes, so what? What's the matter?" I ask.

"Oh, Dennis, something terrible has happened!" Her crying turns to deep full sobs. "You see, after you failed to appear at the trial, a warrant was issued. By your failure to respond to the warrant, you became a fugitive." She continues sobbing.

"So what. That all happened thirty-five years ago!"

She picks her head up. She looks at me and says, "You don't understand. Failure to respond to a warrant is a capital offense. You could be executed for it. You *will* be executed for it. The case was described in the Law News today. Apparently someone turned Tomasso in. Your name wasn't mentioned, but I doubt that it will take more than a week before the authorities are knocking on our door."

I shake my head in disbelief. I prop Janet up against a lounging cushion and make her repeat the story again and again until I can comprehend it.

The situation is ludicrous. I have turned Tomasso in and the whole things boomerangs. I cannot bring myself to tell Janet that it was I; it would mean explaining too many other things, too many things that had best be left unexplained.

And now I am to be under sentence of death for having failed to appear as a witness to testify in a case more than thirty years ago. The sentence is no different for me than for Tomasso, the culprit.

"Janet," I say, "couldn't I plead the unfairness of it all? Couldn't I get off that way?"

"I wish that was a hopeful route," she responds. "Unfortunately, it isn't. The new law is quite clear. Retroactive crimes are permitted. New crimes can carry any penalties the government decides to place on them. It makes no difference that when committed the act wasn't a crime, you can still be punished. It does seem unfair. It *is* unfair. But the law serves many functions. Unfortunately, one of those functions is population control. Retroactive capital punishment is our form of legalized Russian roulette. It is a necessary game, however it's played."

We talk into the night about solutions. Neither of us can find any. Finally Janet grows weary. I am left alone on the lounging cushion

I stare out into the night. The lights of the neighboring towers flicker. I concentrate deeply on them and I find my consciousness ebbing. The room dissolves into white and in my mind the whiteness becomes cold and wet. I remember snow and the comfort of ice, and soon my mind is quiet.

When I finally awake, it is late in the morning. Janet has left for the office and has scrawled a note, "See you later, Love, J."

See you later, I think. Yes, later, much later

I have no trouble making the amfocrapht arrangements. My secret is not yet known. No restrictions have been placed on my travel yet

It has all been too much, not just the technology, but the society, the whole environment I think, while the amfocrapht carries me back to Hudson Bay. I will go back to sleep for a while to that cold deep sleep I enjoyed at Hudson Bay and I'll tell them to wake me when it is over

PLANET FINDERS

VERN DERMOTT

e first man to reach a new planet, provided he filed
a claim for the minerals or–a new life form,
uld take possession. The gamble had paid off, in
that many new planets had been discovered.
he competition had been more than fierce: many
adventurers had been lost in the process.
Now Ted Bicks had actually found an earth type
net, but wasn't certain he could surive to colonize it!

12499—$1.25

LOOK BACK TO EARTH

BY DON PFEIL
WILLIAM BYRNE HAD A MISSION.
FREE FIFTY PLANETS AND
A HUNDRED BILLION PEOPLE.
OR DIE TRYING.

☐ 15299 ★ $1.50

THE BUILDING OF VENUS FOUR

CALDER WILLINGHAM

THE BEST SELLING AUTHOR OF
END AS A MAN AND RAMBLING ROSE
TAKES A BITING LOOK
AT AMERICAN MORES IN A
DEVASTATINGLY FICTIONAL TALE
OF AMBITION, SEXUAL ABSURDITY
IN THE FUNNIEST, TRAGIC,
MOST SENSUALLY STRAIGHT FACED
STORY OF THIS GENERATION.

☐ 22111 ★ $2.25
